"What the hell's going on down there?"

Bolan pitched his voice to sound panicky. "Somebody's coming in through the tunnel. Tomasso's dead, and I don't see Manny. I'm pinned!"

The warrior let off a 3-round burst, then moaned in a convincing imitation of a wounded man. He heard cursing at the top of the stairs and someone muttering about "the dumb son of a bitch getting wasted."

The Executioner ended the man's complaining by launching himself up the stairs, firing on the run. Three gunners on the landing were caught in a hailstorm of 9 mm lead. One flew backward, dead, and a second dived down the stairs, rolling toward the door to the pistol range. The third ran for his life.

Bolan bounded down the stairs, grimly determined to take out the two men before they could raise the alarm. Suddenly the warrior felt himself lifted and thrown back up the stairs, propelled by an explosion.

Gurrola's arsenal had blown.

MACK BOLAN®

The Executioner

DON PENDLETON'S
THE EXECUTIONER®
FEATURING MACK BOLAN®

CHICAGO PAYOFF

A GOLD EAGLE BOOK FROM
WORLDWIDE®

TORONTO • NEW YORK • LONDON • PARIS
AMSTERDAM • STOCKHOLM • HAMBURG
ATHENS • MILAN • TOKYO • SYDNEY

First edition January 1991

ISBN 0-373-61145-5

Special thanks and acknowledgment to
Roland Green for his contribution to this work.

Printed in U.S.A.

He that's secure is not safe.

> —Benjamin Franklin,
> August 1748

The people's safety is the highest law.

> —Anonymous

Life can't be made safe. The world isn't like that. But it can be made safer for the prey, and more dangerous for the predators. I make it my business.

> —Mack Bolan

THE
MACK BOLAN®
LEGEND

Nothing less than a war could have fashioned the destiny of the man called Mack Bolan. Bolan earned the Executioner title in the jungle hell of Vietnam.

But this soldier also wore another name—Sergeant Mercy. He was so tagged because of the compassion he showed to wounded comrades-in-arms and Vietnamese civilians.

Mack Bolan's second tour of duty ended prematurely when he was given emergency leave to return home and bury his family, victims of the Mob. Then he declared a one-man war against the Mafia.

He confronted the Families head-on from coast to coast, and soon a hope of victory began to appear. But Bolan had broken society's every rule. That same society started gunning for this elusive warrior—to no avail.

So Bolan was offered amnesty to work within the system against terrorism. This time, as an employee of Uncle Sam, Bolan became Colonel John Phoenix. With a command center at Stony Man Farm in Virginia, he and his new allies—Able Team and Phoenix Force—waged relentless war on a new adversary: the KGB.

But when his one true love, April Rose, died at the hands of the Soviet terror machine, Bolan severed all ties with Establishment authority.

Now, after a lengthy lone-wolf struggle and much soul-searching, the Executioner has agreed to enter an "arm's-length" alliance with his government once more, reserving the right to pursue personal missions in his Everlasting War.

1

The security guard was bored, and he tried to fight the feeling. He was already so sleepy that it wouldn't take much for him to nod right off.

Then he'd be in trouble. If he got fired from this job, the agency might take a close look at his files. There was stuff in there that couldn't stand that kind of look. Then he'd be through not just with the agency, but maybe with security work completely.

Better to get his butt chewed for going for coffee than to get it kicked off the job for sleeping. He finished his circuit of the warehouse and cut down the center aisle, past the parked forklifts, toward the front office.

He hurried, though he didn't think it was likely that anybody from the head office would be dropping by tonight. Nor anybody from anywhere, for that matter. Who the hell could be interested in a fertilizer warehouse in downstate Illinois, halfway to nowhere and six miles from the nearest bar?

The guard was too busy feeling sorry for himself to detect the faint sound made as a black-clad figure slipped out from the forklifts. He did hear a single footstep behind him, but by then it was too late.

The butt end of a pistol took him behind the left ear as he started to turn. The Smith & Wesson Police Model .38 he'd drawn clattered to the floor, and he fell unconscious on top of it.

MACK BOLAN, the Executioner, checked the security guard's pulse. At the same time he listened for other signs of life in the warehouse.

The guard was alive, and with luck he'd be left with nothing worse than a headache. Bolan wasn't sure that the man knew what went on in this warehouse. If he didn't, he deserved another chance.

Apart from the breathing of the two men, the warehouse was as silent as a tomb, which was what the warrior had expected. The people who used this warehouse to turn industrial fertilizer into illegal explosives relied on secrecy.

This was the small-town Midwest. If they brought in a mob of hardmen from out of town, they would increase security for about two days, until somebody noticed the strangers.

This night the Executioner's target was the stored explosives. Particularly the explosives scheduled for shipment to Chicago, then from Chicago to the East Coast and from there to Ireland. The IRA had plans for those explosives, plans that included killing innocent people. Bolan intended to make those plans a little harder to execute—and that wasn't the only headache he planned to give the predators around Chicago.

With practiced, catlike agility the Executioner pulled himself up on top of a six-foot pile of bags. Using an infrared flashlight and infrared goggles, he checked labels. Good enough. This wasn't a pile of explosives, but high-grade industrial fertilizer would also respond to the charges he was carrying. He pulled four of them out of the pockets of his blacksuit and thrust them through the plastic of the fertilizer bags.

He'd just started setting the timers on the detonators when he heard an unwelcome sound—a truck was backing up to the rear loading dock.

Bolan flattened himself on the bags and waited. If the truck was picking up a legitimate order, he'd just have to wait until it was safely on its way. But at two o'clock in the morning...

The dock door squealed and rattled open. There were four of them, all dressed in work clothes, and three carried Uzis. Two o'clock in the morning was a fine time to visit the warehouse if you were the kind whose work couldn't stand the light of day.

The kind the Executioner had sworn to destroy.

The only question now was timing the explosion to catch the visitors without catching himself or the guard. Bolan held a plan of the warehouse in his memory, which he consulted.

A minute later he'd finished setting the timers. He rolled toward the edge of the pile, then froze as a harsh voice shouted, "Somebody's in here! Johnny, Frank, cover the front!"

All the lights went on as Bolan slid off the pile and into the shadows behind it. The visitors had numbers and maybe firepower on their side. The only way to offset them would be to get out the front way before Johnny and Frank could block it.

But the only way to move that fast would be to abandon the unconscious guard. Bolan set that thought aside the moment it came. He couldn't abandon an innocent man to save his own skin.

A gap between two piles of bags was just wide enough for the warrior to squeeze through. He moved in silence until he reached the end of the gap. From there, the nearest forklift was only six feet away. More important, he had a clear shot at the overhead light.

Bolan raised his Beretta 93-R and fired two rounds into the light, plunging the room into darkness.

The men at the rear door cursed, then started to cough and gag as a CS grenade landed at their feet and released its contents. The gas might take the fight out of the men; it would certainly drive them into the open air. It would also destroy visibility in the forklift aisle.

The gas was prickling at Bolan's eyes and nose as he leaped into the nearest forklift. He pulled it out of the line, crouched so that the entire engine and lift machinery protected him and started rolling.

Bullets flew overhead and ricocheted off the floor into fertilizer bags. Bolan was just as glad now that the explosives were well inside the piles. If a bullet slammed into a demolition charge, it might be an abrupt and noisy ending to Bolan's fight.

The warrior slouched lower as he saw Johnny and Frank crouched at the entrance to the office, which led to the front door.

Then he opened the forklift's engine wide, pointed it at the office and rolled out of the seat. The vehicle charged down the aisle straight at the two gunmen. Against a human opponent they might have held their ground, but against a machine...

They broke, one left, one right. Bolan put a 3-round burst into the man on the left. He hit the floor as the forklift rammed into the office. Wood splintered, glass crashed and the second gunner gave a horrible bubbling scream.

Bolan saw that one of the fork's prongs had rammed through his abdomen, and the guy was pinned to what was left of the office partition like a butterfly in a display case.

The man fainted as Bolan reached the unconscious security guard. No, not unconscious anymore. A ricocheting bullet had gouged away the back of his head. Innocent or not, it no longer mattered if he escaped the explosion.

Bolan checked his watch. Four minutes to go, and two opponents still fighting fit. He vaulted the forklift, his boots crunching glass and wood splinters as he landed in the ruined office. Then he was out the front door and heading around toward the rear, the Beretta up and ready and set for 3-round bursts.

The other two gunmen disappeared into the dark, gas-ridden interior, disinclined to abandon their friends.

Their courage didn't save them, or let them get off more than two shots before 9 mm tumblers cut them down. Bolan rammed a fresh magazine into the Beretta and leaped for the cab of the truck.

Three minutes to go. The vehicle's engine whined and coughed, but refused to turn over. Flooded? Bolan didn't have time to guess. He got out of the cab faster than he'd gone in and sprinted for the gate in the barbed-wire fence that surrounded the warehouse.

It was closed but not locked. He flung it open, barely missing a stride, and kept running. Every extra yard he put between himself and the warehouse—

The quiet countryside erupted as if someone had thrown a switch. Bolan had just enough time to plunge into a drainage ditch before the blast struck. Leaves, twigs, small branches and whole bushes flew overhead, along with bits of wire, fragments of the pickup truck and no doubt pieces of five human bodies. Bolan tasted mud and grass, and the pressure of the shock waves squeezed hard at his ears even though he had his mouth open.

The Executioner waited until the last flying bits struck the ground and he could hear again. He climbed out of the ditch and looked back toward the warehouse as he brushed mud and slime off his blacksuit.

Where the warehouse had been was a vast cloud of smoke, already high enough to blot out most of the battered treetops and some of the stars. Dim flames glowed in the smoke, but gave hardly any light.

All the customers waiting for their bombs were going to be waiting quite a while. While they waited, the innocent would go about their lives with one less danger hanging over them.

Life couldn't be made safe; the world wasn't like that. But it could be made safer for the prey, and more dangerous for the predators.

Bolan fell into a steady jog and headed toward his car, occasionally looking at his watch. Before anyone arrived to investigate the explosion, he'd be in Decatur. Before anyone suspected it wasn't an accident, he'd be on a commuter flight to Chicago.

2

Ramon Villegas was dying the night they killed him.

This was nothing new for him. He'd said at least once a month since he was sixteen, "We're all dying the moment we're born. It just takes some of us longer than others to finish the job."

This got Ramon a heavy reputation as a philosopher among his friends and relatives. He never thought he deserved it. Anyone could look around the neighborhood on the South Side of Chicago and know that life was just a form of dying.

Once it had housed stockyard workers, who worked hard, played hard and often died young but honestly. Then the stockyards moved to Omaha, the last of the stockyard workers went with them and other people moved in.

Now the people of the neighborhood often didn't work at all. They played hard when they could afford to, but they often couldn't. A lot of them still died young, but not honestly—gang fights; bar fights; teenage girls dying in childbirth because no doctor saw them until they went into labor; alcoholism; traffic accidents, when drunk drivers plowed across crowded sidewalks.

And drugs. Anything and everything, but particularly crack. Crack, the street form of cocaine. For fifteen dollars Ramon Villegas would sell you enough to make you forget that life was a form of dying. If you were lucky enough to have fifty, he'd sell you enough to make you really die.

That was another reason Ramon Villegas knew that living and dying weren't far apart. He'd helped quite a few people over the gap. Not deliberately, of course. When he wanted to kill someone, he had a Colt Commander and a Winchester shotgun for the job. But if somebody had the money and didn't care how much of the deadly white powder they took in—well, it wasn't Ramon Villegas's job to tell them to stop.

Villegas was carrying the Commander and a cheap fiberglass suitcase full of crack when he knocked on the door of the old frame house. A respectable Victorian middle-class home, it had been built only a few years after the Chicago fire. After that, for two generations it was a rooming house for stockyard workers.

Now it was Ramon Villegas's crack shack. The people who worked there were *his* people. The crack they handed out was *his* crack. And the money the dead-alive users handed over was *his* money.

Most of it, anyway. He had a reputation for being generous to the people who ran the house. They all made every day what it would have taken them a week to earn at a fast-food restaurant or sweeping floors. No taxes, no Social Security, none of that shit.

Sometimes he'd even give credit to a customer. Particularly if she was a good-looking woman, and sometimes even if she wasn't so good-looking but had some fancy tricks. Like the one who called herself Lady Siggy. She must be right up on forty, but could she turn a man on.

Villegas was wondering if Lady Siggy might be coming in tonight as he climbed the rickety front steps. He also kept looking around. Most of the other dealers in the area had the word that if you messed with Ramon Villegas, bad shit would come down on you real fast. But there was always some asshole who didn't get the word.

Somebody must have been watching inside. Villegas saw a light behind the fish-eye and heard a voice.

"Toledo."

"Tulsa," he replied.

Latches snicked, chains clinked and the door opened. Gordo the Cat was waiting, sneakers crunching fallen plaster every time he shifted position. His old Colt .45 was in his left hand.

"You got the stuff, Ray?"

"No, this is just a social call. I just love to drive around this neighborhood. So scenic. So charming. So fucking easy to get your car ripped off."

"Yeah, come on. You know the Ghost's safe like she was in Fort Knox. You've got a pretty heavy rep, man."

Villegas grinned at the flattery, which was also the truth. Everybody knew that you didn't mess with the Ghost, his purple Mustang, because that was messing with him.

Villegas handed over the suitcase. Gordo opened it and counted the plastic packets. "How long's this supposed to last?"

"Three, four days. There's some more coming down the pipe, but it's not here yet. Why? Business pickin' up?"

"Yeah. Let's hope it stays that way." Gordo handed the suitcase to Luisa, his girlfriend, who actually handed the stuff out upstairs.

Luisa wiggled her way upstairs, with Villegas following her wiggles with his dark eyes. Not bad, not bad at all—but not for him. She was Gordo's.

"We got a problem?"

"Maybe. Sebbie Garcia—I've seen him hanging out around here. Three, four times in the last week."

"Shit."

"That's what he is, all right."

Sebbie Garcia had worked the shack until the day he took a girl's baby as a payment for a double dose of crack. Villegas kicked Garcia's butt down the front steps and sent the baby back. Somebody got the story to the papers, and for a couple of days Ramon Villegas looked like Mr. Nice Guy.

As usual, the papers had it wrong. Villegas wasn't being nice. He just didn't want the hassle with the city that putting the baby out for foster care would give him.

Gordo shrugged. "I told him the next time I see him, nobody's goin' to see him at all after that."

"You wasted your breath, 'stead of wasting him. Gordo, I thought you were smarter than that." A thought struck Villegas. "Or is he running with somebody else now?"

"I can't get a word out of the Rainbows. They say no way. You'll have to talk to the Jaguars."

Villegas nodded. He and the two biggest local gangs left one another alone, because anything else would get a lot of people killed. He'd be one of them before it was over, but the gangs would lose a lot of members, too. Then somebody else would come on the turf and clean up.

"I'm not going to waste time talking to the Jaguars. The next time either of us sees Sebbie, it's the last. Understand?"

"Sure, man. Now, you want some good news for a change?"

"Try me."

"Lady Siggy came in, 'bout ten minutes ago. Gave her from, like, my private stock. She's goin' to be real hot by the time you get upstairs."

Villegas laughed. "That's another reason Sebbie's dead. We had to talk about him when I could've been upstairs with Siggy."

He unzipped his chino jacket, tossed it on a three-legged end table by the stained wall and took the stairs two at a time.

DANNY LIPARDO LOOKED behind him to see the darkened Buick swing around the corner onto Eighteenth Street and out of sight. Snake would keep the car moving real nice, making it appear as if he were just cruising. No way any lookout was going to get suspicious.

In the shadows of the porch of the house next to Villegas's crack shack, Lipardo pulled on his dark red ski mask. His partner, Jimmy "The Bedbug" Vennera, kept an eye on Sebastian Garcia. Not a gun, just an eye—but Garcia knew how fast the Bedbug could draw.

Then it was Vennera's turn to mask up. While he did that, Lipardo pulled out an Ingram submachine gun and held it on Garcia.

Garcia just stared silently at the business end of the weapon. In fact, it seemed as if the whole neighborhood was silent, holding its breath, waiting for the action to start. Somewhere a long way off Lipardo heard what might have been salsa music, and a truck whirred by on Eighteenth Street. Otherwise they might have all been ghosts, deaf to the living world.

"Okay, Garcia. You know what to do. You know what happens if you don't do it. Be smart. When I say go—"

From behind the crack shack came a thump, a clatter and curses in Spanish. Lipardo nearly hit the trigger by sheer reflex. Then he heard the expected *whomp* of gasoline catching fire, and light poured down the alley.

"Go!"

Garcia sprinted across the alley, vaulted the sagging wire fence around the shack's yard and bounded up the stairs, Lipardo and Vennera moved more carefully, not taking their eyes off either Garcia or the front door. Both of them had their Ingrams ready, each with double "tape and turn" magazines.

"Hey, let me in, for Christ's sake!" they heard Garcia shouting. "The Jaguars are on the way."

Normally Gordo the Cat wouldn't have been caught off-guard that way. But the Jaguars had a heavy reputation, and he was starting to smell smoke from the back of the house. The old paint and older wood might have caught fast even without the gasoline. With a gallon of lead-free to help them along, they were going good.

Gordo opened the door. Garcia dived as two bursts of 9 mm rounds whipped overhead, chewing Gordo's face and chest apart. The two masked men sprinted up the front walk and into the hall.

As they hit the plaster, Ramon Villegas bounded down the stairs, naked except for his undershirt and his Commander. At that moment, Garcia started to get to his feet. Villegas's last thought must have been that Garcia had shot Gordo.

The Commander put three .45 rounds into Garcia's head. His body flopped for a bit, then lay still among the plaster that was quickly turning red.

Villegas's concentrating on Garcia gave the two hitters the time they needed. Two more bursts chased each other up the stairs, and stitched Ramon Villegas from throat to stomach, slamming him back against the wall at the bend of the stairs. He slumped to one side, blood running out of his mouth. A blond woman appeared at the top of the stairs and screamed, and the two hitters backed out the door.

On the front steps they met their rear man, holding a Four Roses bottle. "Enough gas left over to make a real nice little Molotov cocktail," the man said. "Want me to try it?"

By now the flames in the rear of the house were leaping above the roof. Smoke was pouring out of the front windows, and the hitters heard screams from upstairs.

"Nah," Lipardo said. "We got what we came for." He didn't much care if the women saved themselves or burned to death. It was a lot more important to get out of there before somebody called the fire department.

The Buick screeched around the corner on two wheels. Another screech, and it stopped by the alley, the rear doors already popping open.

The three men went over the fence like kangaroos. The Buick burned rubber and took off down the street. If anybody saw the license number, they managed to forget it.

By the time the firemen showed up, the house was a total loss—as were Ramon Villegas, Gordo the Cat and Sebbie Garcia. The customers were luckier. None of them had anything worse than smoke inhalation, minor burns and the problem of finding out where they were going to get their next hit of crack.

BOLAN GOT OFF THE COMMUTER plane at O'Hare International Airport just as the airport was coming to life. The last passengers from red-eye flights were deplaning, and the coffee shops were opening to keep them alive.

That gave Bolan a little extra cover, in case anyone was waiting for him unexpectedly. He still went through the full routine of covering his tracks.

He got his shoes shined in a men's room in another terminal while he waited for his baggage to reach the terminal where he'd deplaned. He boarded one rent-a-car shuttle bus, transferred to a second halfway across the airport, then walked back to the nearest taxi stand.

The taxi took him to a hotel in a six-hotel complex attached to a convention center five miles from the airport. Bolan waited until the taxi was out of sight and the doorman had his back turned, then cut across an acre of manicured lawn.

He finally checked into the cheapest of the six hotels. It didn't have the best security, but for one night and after thoroughly covering his tracks, it should do.

The hotel coffee shop was open, so he went in and ordered a breakfast he figured even the worst cook couldn't ruin. He was almost right.

When he got back to his room, it was time to call Hal Brognola.

The big man from Justice came right on the line.

"Stage one, free and clear," Bolan growled.

"Good. The Decatur and Illinois State Police are already making noises about an accident. I suspect our bomb peddler doesn't have as many friends as he thought."

"At least not anymore." Bolan summarized the raid on the warehouse.

"Okay," Brognola said. "Now, the next stage was going to be your Chicago contacts. But we might have a slight problem there." The big Fed sounded as if he had a cold, but that was probably only the electronic security devices on his telephone at Stony Man Farm.

Brognola described the takedown of a crack shack on Chicago's South Side the night before. "Ramon Villegas was nobody's Mr. Nice Guy," he concluded. "But he had been on good terms with the Instituto de Fraternidad."

"The Lirio family's contribution to the less fortunate of the city?"

"Yeah. Also, the director of the institute is a guy named Ignacio Luna. He has a brother in the Violent

Crimes unit named Carlos Luna. Carlos Luna is one of your contacts.''

"Any danger Luna's on the take?"

"Negative. The only thing is, if somebody's sniffing around the institute, Carlos might have worries we hadn't expected."

"No argument. Who're my other contacts?"

"One of them's an old friend of yours—a certain lady named Rose. The other's an undercover cop by the name of Alfredo Guzman. From the file, he seems straight. He sounds like a bit of a loose cannon, but we need his connections. I won't ask you to work with him if you think there'll be a problem. But give him a chance."

"Don't worry, Hal. Give me twenty-four hours to see what I can come up with on Villegas and his tie to the institute."

"Done."

3

Mack Bolan kept his feet out from under the table in the back room of the squalid little bar and grill, which would allow a quicker getaway. But there was another reason. He suspected that under the table were cockroaches the size of tennis balls. He had managed to avoid stepping on several as Alfredo Guzman led him to the back room.

"Where's Sergeant Luna?" the warrior asked when the waitress had slapped two drinks onto the table and left.

Guzman didn't touch his glass, shrugging instead. "I don't put a tracer on him every time he doesn't show up for a meet."

Bolan swung around in his chair and looked from Guzman to the exit and back again. "I don't play games. I suspect it isn't in your orders, either."

"I write my own orders, friend." From what Brognola had said, that wasn't bravado. It was the simple truth. Guzman got results either because of or in spite of his methods. Since nobody knew which, nobody felt like reining him in and ending the results.

"Maybe you do. But then, maybe you know what's in them. It could even help if you told me." Bolan stood. "I know it would hurt quite a lot if you didn't."

Guzman picked up his drink, sipped it and looked Bolan up and down. The warrior noticed that the undercover cop was careful to keep his free hand in plain sight.

"Okay," Guzman said. "You want to know where Carlos is?"

"If it's not too much trouble." Bolan didn't sit down.

"He's talking with his brother, following up a hunch. The hunch is that Ramon Villegas's connections with the Insituto de Fraternidad had something to do with his getting wasted. So who better to talk to than the director of the institute, particularly when he's your brother?"

"You sound like you think there might be somebody better."

"Not bad, not bad." Guzman saw Bolan's eyes narrow and shift toward the exit again. "Sorry. I'll cut out the jokes and get on with the business.

"Carlos is following up the hunch with permission from his boss, Captain Gallery of Violent Crimes. If that hunch doesn't pay off, the Villegas case goes into the routine gang-slaying file."

There it would stay, if Bolan knew the way the average overworked and understaffed big-city police force worked. Solving it would need a piece of luck, like the murderer walking into the station in broad daylight.

Bolan sat down. "Okay. Except that somehow I have the feeling that if Sergeant Luna can't do anything, it's your turn."

"Give the big man a— Sorry, again."

"Maybe you should try for fewer apologies and more explanations."

"Okay. *Maybe* I can do something. I've been promoted from runner to soldier in Jorge Langas's crew. If you've never heard of them, don't sweat it. They're pretty small potatoes, and nothing at all outside Chicago."

Bolan not only hadn't heard of the Langas gang. He hadn't heard that Guzman had penetrated any gang at all. But then a security-conscious undercover officer probably wouldn't mention that fact anywhere Hal Brognola might have heard it.

He wasn't surprised, either, that Guzman could pass as a criminal. At the moment, he looked as if he spent all his time in the back room of roach-ridden bars. But the photograph Bolan had seen of him showed him in a three-piece suit, looking as if he owned half of Chicago's Loop.

Guzman could fit in anywhere, without anybody asking questions. Even if they thought of it, they might keep their mouths shut. The man was a head shorter than Bolan but every bit as broad across the shoulders. He looked and moved like somebody you didn't want to annoy by asking questions he didn't want to answer.

"What's the Langas racket?"

"Prostitution and porno. Kiddie stuff, too." Bolan made a face. Guzman nodded. "Yeah. Thing is, they've got some sort of deal going with the Vitellis."

"I've heard of them."

"I'll bet you have."

On one of Bolan's previous trips to Chicago, the Vitelli white-slave operation had been his principal target. Several members of the Family and many of their soldiers hadn't survived the Executioner's cleansing flame.

But Mafia Families or any other kind of criminal organization were like sharks—they could be cut to pieces, and not only wouldn't they die, but they'd still be dangerous.

"Suppose I hit the Vitellis?"

"You thinking of finishing some unfinished business?"

"Let's say I'm a man who doesn't like loose ends." Bolan sipped enough of his drink to be polite, then stood.

"You've got the message-drop number. Use it as soon as you hear from Sergeant Luna. Then try to set up another meeting for all three of us."

"Can do."

Guzman had his feet up on the table and was shouting for a second drink as Bolan went out the back way.

THE COCKROACHES IN THE BACK room of the Instituto de Fraternidad weren't under the table. They were on the ceiling.

What was under the table was silverfish, mice and a lot of incredibly dirty vinyl tile.

"I thought you had plenty of volunteers to keep this place clean," Carlos Luna complained.

His brother, Ignacio, shrugged. "We try to get them through here and out into the world as fast as we can. Or at least as fast as Immigration and Naturalization will let us."

Carlos nodded. One of these days the Immigration and Naturalization Service would be efficient, civilized and quick at processing people. The day after that, Captain Gallery would have a sex-change operation.

Meanwhile, there was this morning's coffee break, and the institute did have first-class coffee. Carlos held out his cup for a refill.

"We're going to have a coffee problem as well as a housecleaning one in another week," Ignacio said. "Laura's been cooking since she got her papers. Now we've found her a job out in Palos Heights. No way she's going to commute back here to keep us in coffee."

"Look on the bright side, Ignacio," Carlos said. "If the next cook makes real horse-piss, you can leave it out for the silverfish."

"I wish we could." Ignacio sighed, running a hand across a sweaty forehead and through tangled black hair. "The little bastards think our files are real gourmet treats." He ran his hand back through his hair in an unsuccessful effort to repair the damage and stared at his brother.

"Maybe it's time for a straight answer. Is this a social call, or business? You run into another bird with a busted wing you want us to help?"

"Hey, come on. I only did that twice. Not like Ramon Villegas. He must have sent you twenty, twenty-five. Remember Carlotta, that runaway? She couldn't have been much more than fourteen...."

Carlos had a rare talent. He could talk for half an hour about something, sneaking in leading questions at five-minute intervals. While he talked, he could also watch the man he was talking to.

It wasn't something he liked doing to his brother, but since yesterday he'd realized something else. He might not be the only one who thought Ignacio knew something about Ramon Villegas.

"It doesn't look like Villegas is going to be sending us any more people," Ignacio said finally. He almost interrupted his brother, and there was a lot more sweat on his forehead than before. That could be the poor air-conditioning, but still . . .

"Maybe this is none of my business," Carlos began, "but did anybody at the institute ever object to Villegas? I suppose everybody knew he was dealing—"

"No," Ignacio said abruptly. Too abruptly.

"Not even grumbling into their coffee?"

"Hey, brother, this is too much business. What do you think—somebody at the institute took him out?"

It was supposed to be a joke, and Ignacio was even close to smiling. But Carlos had known his brother's real smiles for thirty years. This wasn't one of them.

He still had to treat the joke like a real one. He hoped his laughter didn't sound fake.

"No way. At least not any of your staff. But what about the people Villegas sent? Did they all stay clean?"

"Well, I'd have to look them up in the files the silverfish haven't eaten. I know we've got one of them crashing here since last week. A kid named Willy Lopez. He was a busboy in a restaurant, the old Playa Roja, until he decided to join the Army. Boss canned him, so he's here until he goes down to Fort Benning next month.''

Carlos almost laughed. His brother was playing back the same trick used on him—a flow of chatter to see how the other man would react.

"Mind if I look at the records?"

"Not without a court order. Sorry, but I gotta go by the rules. Some of the people around here haven't been real straight all the time. They deserve a chance to stay straight without cops looking over their shoulders."

"Even your baby brother?"

"Even my baby brother." The tone was light, but now Ignacio wasn't even pretending to smile.

Carlos decided that he really didn't want a family fight over this business.

Time to go back to Captain Gallery and tell him that they'd have to follow up the hunch some other way. It was a good hunch. Carlos was sure of that. But all hunches weren't created equal, at least as far as what you could do about them.

DANNY LIPARDO ADJUSTED his ear protectors, turned downrange and raised the Korth Combat Magnum in his left hand.

The stainless-steel revolver had cost him more than two thousand dollars the previous year. But the year before that, he had become top soldier to Don Hector Gurrola. He could afford such little luxuries, as long as they worked, too.

The Korth certainly was no expensive toy. Shooting left-handed, Lipardo put all six .357 Magnum rounds into a five-inch circle. Shooting with a more standard grip, he could hold a two-inch circle at twenty-five yards.

Lipardo stepped back and let Jimmy Vennera take his turn. The Colt Python that the man used was, to Lipardo, a poor man's gun. But then Vennera was better with steel than with lead.

A man looking at the two gunners might have taken them for brothers. A woman looking at them would have dismissed Lipardo instantly as the fool of the family. Vennera, on the other hand, she would have wanted to get to know better. Something dangerous lurked behind those dark eyes....

Both men were careful to go on making those impressions. It had helped in the past; it would help in the future that Lipardo wanted to discuss, here in the pistol range built off the Lirios' underground fallout shelter.

The pistol range was a closely guarded secret. It had to be, in a suburb where even owning a pistol was a crime. Lipardo found that amusing. He could have named people within six blocks who did everything from snorting cocaine to molesting their own teenage sons.

The two men each shot off eighteen more rounds, then removed their ear protectors and began to clean their weapons.

"What next?" Vennera asked.

Lipardo smiled. "You mean 'who,' don't you?"

"Well, I suppose I do."

"Don't be too eager. It won't be a woman."

Vennera muttered something obscene. Lipardo shrugged. "The world has both, you know."

"Yes, but for pleasure—"

"I've seen you as happy over hunting a man as over hunting a woman."

"Hunting, yes. But not catching." Vennera sighed. "What will be, will be. Who is it?"

"Willy Lopez. It seems that he knows too much."

"Ah. Then we take the Playa Roja?"

"Only the manager. And *we* do not even take him."

"Ah."

"Stop pretending more respect than you feel," Lipardo said sharply. "It's simple. The Vitellis have long since . . . 'made their bones' is the old phrase. It's time for Don Jorge Langas to do the same, to prove his loyalty. It has to look like angry friends of Lopez blame the owner for his death. In their rage they'll kill the manager. Only the 'friends' will be Langas's soldiers."

"Indeed. That should be a job even they can handle. And when they have done so, they will think they are as much in our favor as the Vitellis?"

"In Don Hector Gurrola's favor. Always say it that way, even to yourself."

Lipardo and his partner had long since decided that they could rule Gurrola's little empire far better than the man himself. But that decision had to be kept secret until they had the strength to move. Recruiting the Vitellis had given them part of that strength. The Langas soldiers might give them the rest.

But Gurrola himself was still capable of giving them anonymous graves if he learned their plans too soon. The connection with the Lirio family went through him, and he still had loyal soldiers, as well as Lirio money.

Lipardo pulled a Polaroid snapshot from the pocket of his cardigan sweater, which showed a remarkably handsome young Hispanic woman in the uniform of a captain in the United States Army, and she wore pilot's wings.

"Ah, the latest picture of La Principesa?"

"Exactly, and don't let that look cross your face again."

"Not even with you?"

"Not even with me. She's coming home for nearly a month this time, and she's more likely to notice anything suspicious, such as you leering at her."

"Is Don Hector still thinking with his balls?"

"I don't doubt it. Even if he isn't, Angelita Lirio is still old Don Salvador's pride and joy. He won't strike back the way Gurrola will. But it will make trouble, offending him. To make trouble this close to the end—"

"I'm not a fool, Danny."

"Then don't behave like one."

"My word of honor."

Gurrola still hoped to marry Angelita Lirio. Although perhaps it would help if he succeeded in doing so. Lipardo wondered if there was anything he could do to help.

Maybe there was. But it wouldn't be good, in the long run. Salvador Lirio didn't have long to live. His fortune was large, so that even divided among several heirs, it would make Angelita a very wealthy woman. Gurrola would have all the money necessary to hire anyone he needed.

If so, he might decide he didn't need Danny Lipardo or Jimmy Vennera. Lipardo was prepared to sacrifice his partner, if necessary, but he would rather do that *after* he ruled the Gurrola empire, not before.

4

Wearing combat black and rigged for war, Mack Bolan kept out of the pools of street light as he stalked toward the Instituto de Fraternidad. It was too late for respectable citizens and too early for the gangs, but if no one at all saw him, so much the better.

This was supposed to be a soft probe of the institute, to see if Villegas had left any sort of trail. Not a trail to his criminal connections—everyone knew the score there—but a trail that those connections might have followed to the institute. That was something else.

It was also something that Bolan wanted to find without input from the Luna brothers. If Ignacio felt threatened, then Carlos might have to chose between a quarrel with his brother and working with Bolan.

If Luna chose his brother, Bolan would be back to playing a lone hand. He was used to that, but the younger Luna might prove useful on this mission. Good allies weren't to be given up lightly.

The Executioner reached one end of the alley that wound through battered lofts and stores to wind up behind the institute. He looked to either side for tails, overhead for sentries, then down at the rough asphalt of the alley—looked, and frowned. A patch of rotted garbage showed fresh footprints. So fresh that water was still seeping into them from a puddle.

Bolan peered up the alley. It wasn't his imagination. Those faint traces of wet garbage trailed off around the next corner. He flattened himself against a wall, heard bits of dislodged mortar trickle to the pavement and froze with the Beretta in his hand.

Whoever had gone down the alley either hadn't noticed the sound, or had noticed it and also stopped to listen. Bolan waited with a warrior's patience born in the jungles of Vietnam and honed to a razor's edge in a hundred battles since.

Only the sounds of the city broke the night. Bolan listened. One skill he'd learned in the battles since Vietnam was to pick out the faintest human sound from the mechanical din of a city.

Nothing. Whoever had gone down the alley had either gone on or gone to ground, laying an ambush. Bolan snapped the safety off his .44. The Desert Eagle would give him extra range and striking power if the Beretta wasn't enough.

Staying close to the wall, the Executioner catfooted forward.

IGNACIO LUNA WAVED GOODBYE to the institute's two clerks as they reached the street. They didn't see him, and turned east toward their bus stop.

They would probably be the next people to start talking about what was bothering him. He'd always made a point of saying good morning and good-night to everybody, until this business of Ramon Villegas began. Now he'd heard people comparing him to a Toltec idol—fat, dark, ugly and silent.

He didn't care. Words wouldn't hurt. What hurt was not knowing how far the death of Ramon Villegas would take the institute.

No, that wasn't quite the way to put it. What hurt was suspecting that he knew how far things would go, but not being sure. He also suspected that he had no way of being sure. Not even telling everything he knew or suspected to Carlos might be enough.

It would only be enough to bring trouble to the Lirio family, but that would be a crime in itself. Not maybe as great as the crimes of Ramon Villegas or those who killed him, but a crime nonetheless. It would be the crime of taking money away from the people the institute was intended to help, the Mexican immigrants who wanted to make a new home in America but had nothing but a little English and a lot of determination to help them.

Ignacio looked at the papers on his desk. He decided that none of them needed work tonight. A quick tour of the office showed him that nobody was working late. Nobody had slipped in the back door, either, to shoot up in the bathrooms, steal the office equipment or just fall asleep in one of the chairs in the interviewing room.

He set the answering machine, then turned off the lights and opened the door to the street.

DANNY LIPARDO WAITED across the street. He wore jeans, boots and a dirty green jacket. The man was old enough to have a son the age of most street punks, but could pass as one after dark.

That helped when he was on a job like tonight's, where a mask would have made him stand out. Looking like any one of a thousand street machos was a much better disguise.

He watched Ignacio Luna make a great big thing of locking up, and wanted to laugh. If he'd really wanted to get into the institute, there wasn't a lock in the place that could keep him out.

Tonight that job was in the hands of other men. Not as good as he was, not even good enough for Gurrola. But good enough for what he was having them do. They might not learn how much Villegas had told people in the institute, but if they did, it wouldn't matter.

The important work tonight was Ignacio Luna's death, and Lipardo had saved that for himself.

"We'll make it look like an ordinary street crime," he'd explained to the other three men. "The Lirios will understand how even Ignacio's luck might run out on the streets. So will the police.

"But if the man is found dead in the institute, the police will investigate. Perhaps even the Feds will be called in. And they might find out things we don't want them to know."

Which could end up with Hector Gurrola abandoning his whole Chicago operation and starting from scratch somewhere else. Lipardo wasn't absolutely sure that he'd be with Gurrola if that happened. He knew more about the operation than anybody except Don Hector himself. The man might decide that Lipardo was more dangerous as a traitor than he was useful as a hit man.

While Lipardo considered this possibility, Ignacio got the half-block lead he was supposed to get. Lipardo turned up the collar of his jacket and followed.

PARKING A CAR UNDER THE EL tracks wasn't only illegal—usually it was a good way to get the car stolen
or at least vandalized. But Ignacio Luna's parking
place under the El tracks was the safest in the neighborhood, for him. It was right by the back door of
Antonio Boba's grocery and *taquería*. The business
stayed open late, and there was always someone in the
kitchen. If it was old man Boba himself, the car was
as safe as if it had been locked in a garage. The institute bought a lot of its food from Boba at wholesale
prices, and he knew a good customer when he saw
one.

Also, the institute had found a way of getting Boba's
daughter away from a gang boyfriend. Even more,
she'd married the son of one of the institute's board
members. Now she and her husband were living in
Minneapolis and had just given the old man his first
grandson. For the people who had done that for him,
Boba would have done a lot more than watch cars.

Ignacio climbed over the chain stretched along the
sidewalk and picked his way around the puddles. Most
of them were no more than mud patches, but he had
on his only pair of good shoes.

An El train roared overhead, its lights showing Ignacio that his Chevette had company—an ancient
Oldsmobile station wagon, probably abandoned, with
an open tailgate and broken window so he couldn't see
any license plates.

As Ignacio reached his car, he also reached his decision. He'd have to turn anybody's curiosity away
from the institute, or at least the Lirio family. Finding out who killed Ramon Villegas wasn't worth tak-

ing money from the institute. To avenge a criminal by stealing from the honest poor—stupid.

The creak of metal behind Ignacio made him turn. A man in the back of the Oldsmobile raised a gun, and before the director of the institute could open his mouth to shout, the pistol went off.

BOLAN REACHED THE BACK door of the institute knowing he was trailing two men. The double set of footprints was unmistakable.

The back door was closed, but a gentle push told the warrior that it had been left unlocked. Flat against the wall, he waited, the Desert Eagle in hand.

Then, in a single flowing sequence of movements, he whirled, kicked the door open and dived across the threshold.

A shot blazed past his cheek and shattered the wired glass window high in the door. Bolan turned abruptly and found himself too close to a dark-clad figure to raise the Desert Eagle.

He slammed it down instead, where the opponent's gun hand ought to be, and felt bone give under the blow. Then he rammed the heel of his free hand under the man's chin. The guy flew backward into a filing cabinet, which toppled over with a crash.

The second man popped up from behind a desk, an Ingram M-10 held at waist level. Bolan's finger hit the trigger first, even though the hardman got off a burst. But it was the burst of a man with a .44 Magnum slug in his chest, a dying effort.

Both were down and dead. So was any chance of a soft probe. The Instituto de Fraternidad was in for a major scandal. The only thing Bolan could do was to get out before the police came.

The warrior turned to leave. Distant, but unmistakable, he heard three gunshots.

FIRING .44 SPECIALS from a two-and-a-half-inch barrel, the Bulldog had an effective range of something less than twenty-five yards. Since Lipardo was shooting from less than twenty-five feet, he had no problem putting three rounds in Ignacio Luna's chest.

Two of them ripped his heart open. The third shattered ribs, which punctured his lungs. He was killed twice over, but it was the ruined heart that stopped first. Lung spasms sprayed blood out of his mouth, but he was already dead.

Lipardo was bending over Ignacio, reaching for his wallet, when a sense of being watched triggered an alarm. He turned, rolled and came up with his gun aimed at the bulky figure standing gape mouthed in the lighted doorway. Another light above the door spread a dirty yellow pool out under the El tracks, far enough to expose Lipardo.

The newcomer had a good look at him. Too good to let him be able to pass it on to the police.

The Bulldog bucked twice more. The silhouetted target jerked under the impact of the bullets, then toppled backward. Someone screamed, but the screamer didn't come to the door.

Lipardo signaled to his security man. The second hitter had just emerged from the shadows when those same shadows spewed flame.

The security man gave a grunt of surprise and turned. Lipardo didn't have time to stare at the red stain spreading across the man's chest and stomach. He barely had time to duck before more bullets struck the man's head.

Lipardo vaulted over the Oldsmobile's hood and sprinted for the nearest alley. It meant ducking and dodging around the girders of the El, and he could still hear the screaming when he was a block away.

Nobody came after him, though. He had time to drop the Bulldog down a storm drain, then cut back under the El, down another alley and mix with the late-night crowd at a Burger King on Twenty-Fourth Street.

Since the management of the fast-food restaurant was pretty sticky about loitering, he wound up ordering a Coke and fries. He was thirsty, as he always was after a hit, but ordering two Cokes might have stuck in somebody's memory. That was the secret of a good hit. Be part of the scenery, except for the moment when the target was actually being taken down.

After a while Lipardo realized that he was hungry. So he ordered a Whopper to go with his fries, which gave him the excuse he needed for a second Coke.

Getting something in his stomach cleared his head. He decided that this hadn't been such a good hit, after all, unless the two men in the institute had got clear.

BOLAN BROKE EVERY tactical rule, following Ignacio Luna's trail. He was in time to see one of the hit men silhouette himself against the light from the rear of the *taquería*

Snap-shooting got a body hit. Aimed fire put the man down the rest of the way, with 9 mm tumblers from the Beretta. Then a green-jacketed figure was vaulting the Oldsmobile's hood and vanishing into the maze of shadows and steel under the El.

The Executioner couldn't hope to hit him except on full automatic. He didn't dare use that, for the same reason he'd switched from the Desert Eagle to the Beretta. Too many innocent people were too close.

He couldn't even hope to chase the man. In territory the guy probably knew better than the back of his hand, he could lay an ambush wherever he pleased. Worst of all, he could double back and hit the *taquería* again. Reluctantly Bolan holstered the Beretta and walked into the lights. The people drew back, except for those bent over two figures sprawled on the ground in pools of blood.

One of them, the warrior recognized as Ignacio Luna. He also recognized death.

The second man was fatter, older, and by some miracle still alive. Bolan knelt beside him.

"Clean towels or rags, now!" he ordered in Spanish. "Anything to stop the bleeding from his chest."

"Right away," someone replied.

Bolan drew his combat knife and cut away the older man's shirt. it looked like one bullet in the chest, fortunately missing the lungs and heart, and another in the belly.

"Here."

Bolan reached without looking, then began packing the chest wound. The stomach wound was hardly bleeding, which could be good or bad, depending on how much damage the bullet had done inside.

But that would be a doctor's job to find out. All Bolan would hope to do was fight for the man's life until the doctors came.

"DIDN'T GALLERY TAKE you off this case?"

The familiar voice made Carlos Luna look up—not much, because after a sleepless night his head seemed to weigh half a ton, but enough to see a scruffy-looking man standing in front of him.

He hoped the poor bastard hadn't got his hopes up about getting help from the institute. The institute seemed about to draw its last breath.

Maybe the Lirios and their friends could keep the money coming, but without a staff, the money, obviously, wouldn't get disbursed. And without Ignacio, there wouldn't be a staff.

"Hey, man, are you there, or is this *Robocop* and you're the cyborg?"

Luna surged out of the chair, knocking it over. He drew back an arm, ready to punch the joker into silence. Then he recognized the face as well as the voice.

"Alfredo! What the hell are you doing here?"

Guzman shrugged. "I thought I asked that question first."

Luna shook his head again. This time it seemed to weigh only a couple of hundred pounds. Maybe if he got a good night's sleep tonight, it would be back to normal by morning.

Except that Ignacio was getting the kind of sleep you only got in funeral homes. He was never going to be back to normal. Nothing Carlos did would change that. But somehow he had to learn who killed Ignacio and put Boba in the hospital. Somehow he had to make them pay for it. He'd sleep or not, depending on how much sleep helped him accomplish that goal.

Meanwhile a former partner of his was standing in front of him, asking a question that deserved an answer.

"I never got on it," Luna replied wearily. "Personal involvement. You know the rules."

"So I do. I wondered if you did. I also wonder when you last ate."

"Got any place in mind?"

"Ah, the patient is sitting up and taking—"

"Fredo, I might punch you out, after all."

"Hey, sorry. Remember, I knew Ignacio. I even sent him a couple of strays. He was quite a man, and I want to get the people who killed him just as much as you do."

"Really?"

Guzman crossed himself, then looked around the interview room. "I also have a couple of ideas that I'd like to talk over someplace else. Kill two birds with one breakfast, so to speak."

"Toss for who pays?"

"My idea, my tab."

BOLAN SAW IMMEDIATELY that Alfredo Guzman really was a chameleon who could change to match his surroundings. In the back room of the bar and grill he'd looked as if he hadn't slept under a roof in a week.

Now, in the French Quarter dining room of the Palmer House, he looked as if luxury hotels were an everyday part of his life-style.

A polite cough from the waiter reminded Bolan that he'd been staring at the men across the table instead of the menu. He ordered an omelet, and the waiter vanished.

"Sergeant Guzman. You were saying something about a smell in the Langas gang?"

"Just a faint one. I'm working my way up pretty fast, and I'm pretty chummy with a medium-sized...call him a vice prince. Not many girls and not fancy ones, but good cash flow and he's ambitious."

"Any fringe benefits?" Luna asked. His voice was tight, and he looked as if he hadn't slept at all.

"He doesn't like them to wear stuff with fringes. Says it looks cheap. So do they, but what do I know about women?"

"If I answered that question, it would take all morning and we'd be thrown out of here before I finished."

Guzman looked away from his friend. "Hey, I won't do it again. I just get into the habit when I'm working. Nobody suspects the class clown, and when he's good with a knife and a gun—well, you know what happens."

"Yeah. Nothing, until you're ready to put the arm on them. So what's with this vice prince?"

"He's talking about Langas signing on with Gurrola."

"I didn't know Gurrola had that kind of money."

"He doesn't, at least right now. But Prince says he's heard rumors that Gurrola is going to pick up a lot of clean money pretty soon. The rumors don't say where, but they do say something about a lot of it being Hispanic."

To Bolan, that sounded like the Lirio family. And from what Guzman had told him previously about

Danny Lipardo, Gurrola's second-in-command, he wondered if Gurrola had suddenly noticed that the guy had ambitions and decided to do something about it. Like finding a source of cash that didn't depend on Lipardo or his connections.

Bolan was all in favor of Lipardo and Gurrola coming to blows. If Guzman's information about the Langas mob gave the Executioner a way to speed that up...

"I'd have learned more, except that the girls are all of a sudden scared to talk," Guzman went on. "Rumor is that Lipardo had Jimmy 'The Bedbug' Vennera cut one of them up real bad. One of these days, I think I might just pay a little call on the Bedbug and spray him with insect killer."

"Deal me in on that," Luna said.

"Me too," Bolan added. He'd been told that Vennera got his thrills by working over women. Viciously.

"You're on our side?" Luna asked.

"Remember the man I mentioned?" Guzman interjected. "You're looking at him. And if you don't remember that, he's the reason Tony Boba's grandson still has a grandfather. The docs say the old man wouldn't have made it without this guy's doing a patch job on him."

Bolan had the familiar sense of being looked over. Finally Luna frowned. Before he could say anything, the waiter brought their orders.

The frown stayed on the detective's face halfway through the meal. Finally he said, "I thought you were dead. Gone over the edge in Texas, then put away where somebody got to you."

"You're about six rumors out of date," Bolan said lightly. "The Texas business was a frame. Fortunately most of the people behind it won't be bothering anyone again."

"It's really a vendetta with you, isn't it?" Luna asked.

Bolan shrugged. "Vendetta? You've just lost your brother. Think about the same thing happening to your whole family."

After a minute Luna nodded. "I think I understand. But isn't dealing with you a career-buster if I get caught? I've got two more years before my pension's locked in, never mind the promotion."

"You've forgotten Ignacio already?" Guzman asked.

"No, I'm just remembering Maria and Julio. And don't ever say that again, Fredo." Bolan heard steel in Luna's voice.

"Sorry. Me and my smart mouth again. We're not going to bring our friend into headquarters and show him the Villegas file, if that's what you mean. But what we know, he knows. We'll coordinate, so we don't trip up one another, but we won't be a regular team."

"What about Gallery?"

"I have friends in the Justice Department," Bolan said. "They can arrange it so that almost any policeman in the country can look good or bad. If they arrange it so that Gallery gets the headlines for putting Hector Gurrola out of business..."

"Got a number I can call?"

Bolan handed over a business card with a telephone number penciled on the back. "This gets you somebody who can reach somebody in the Justice Department at all times. Don't use it unless it's an emergency, though."

"Like burning candles to Saint Jude?" Guzman said.

"The patron saint of hopeless causes?" Bolan asked. "Don't waste the candles."

5

Mack Bolan awakened the next morning, called Brognola and gave a status report.

"I'll put our computer people on the Lirios right away," Brognola said when Bolan was finished.

Aaron Kurtzman, the Stony Man Farm computer expert, had access to all government files. Or at least he could gain access, if necessary. The warrior suspected that it would be necessary in this case. This operation would be skating fairly close to the line where both the narcotics agents and the FBI claimed jurisdiction. Stepping on their toes was never a good idea.

Bolan's presidential pardon would keep DEA or FBI agents from shooting him on sight. It wouldn't keep them from interfering with his work, until the killers had time to get away.

"How fast?"

"Couple of days. So we've got time to work out a safe drop."

"Good."

Exchanging information securely and reliably was always important. In this affair, it could mean life or death, and for many people who wouldn't be out on the firing line.

"I'll do the regular twenty-four hour call-in," Bolan added. "I'll have Guzman call in again so you can make a voice print for him."

In an emergency Guzman might have to make the call, and they had to have some way of being sure it was really Guzman. Recognition and access codes could be tortured out of almost anybody, but it was hard to disguise a voice well enough to fool Stony Man's main computer or its presiding experts.

"Right. Take care, guy."

HECTOR GURROLA SAT IN a deck chair by the palm tree at the northeast corner of the swimming pool. The sun blinds overhead were open, so he wore only white swimming trunks and gold-framed sunglasses. Danny Lipardo sat in another deck chair, facing his boss.

"I think we have a problem," Gurrola announced. "Fortunately it's one that I can leave to you. One of our rivals clearly has a man almost as good as you in his service. I think you should find who that man is and deal with him."

"Of course, Don Hector. And what about old Boba? I'm ashamed of my poor shooting—"

Gurrola laughed. "We can hardly go into Cook County Hospital and shoot everyone Boba might have talked to. No, let's add this new man to our list, but otherwise go on as we have planned."

The mobster reached into a small leather-covered cigar box on the table beside his chair. Besides cigars, the box held suntan oil, a Browning Hi-Power and a beeper to call the maid.

"The Bedbug gets Willy Lopez?" Gurrola asked when his cigar was drawing well.

"Yes."

"Good. The more he's kept away from the house while I'm gone, the better."

So Don Hector was going ahead with his trip. Lipardo hadn't dared ask where the man was going, but he could guess. If Gurrola could deal directly with the Colombian drug dealers and cut out the Miami middlemen, he'd be able to flood Chicago with cocaine at much lower prices than any rival.

He also might not live to return to Chicago, or even live to reach Colombia, if the mad dogs of Miami learned of his plans. But that was a danger that had to be faced. Both Gurrola and Lipardo could face almost any danger for sufficient profit.

"I have warned him about La Principesa."

"Even better," Gurrola replied. The yearning in his voice was unmistakable. So Don Hector was still besotted with Angelita Lirio.

Well, every man had the right to one weakness, Lipardo thought. If it was a weakness that would strengthen the younger man's position, so much the better.

"I'll also go ahead with sending the Langas men against the Playa Roja," Lipardo said. "They'll pretend to be angry friends of Willy Lopez, of course. If they succeed, the restaurant will need a new manager."

"And if they fail?"

"Then I think we might have to deal with them harshly. If they have no hope of joining us but know too many of our secrets, they become too dangerous."

A maid appeared, put down the two drinks that Gurrola had ordered earlier and curtsied. "Will there be anything else, Don Hector?"

"Not for now, Rita," Gurrola said. Both men watched the maid sway gracefully out of sight.

"If Vennera can't be kept away from the house while La Principesa is here, send him to the maid," Gurrola suggested. "I'm sure she'll be happy to receive him."

Lipardo doubted that the maid would be happy, but she would certainly prefer seeing him to what would happen to her if she complained. The last maid who had complained about Vennera hadn't died at his hands. She'd died by her own, when she saw what he'd done to her.

ROSE'S WATERING HOLE stood on a side street in Oak Park, just west of Chicago. Through the back window above the microwave, Bolan could see the lights of traffic on the expressway that cut through the suburb.

"So what brings you back, Milo?" Rose asked. She was a big woman with blue-black hair beginning to show gray and a figure that didn't show the years nearly as much.

She wore a grin and a purple dress cut to show off that figure. Right now the grin told Bolan that she knew exactly who he really was, but she'd call him by the name he was using because he wanted it that way.

"A couple of things that I want from you," Bolan replied, returning the grin.

"I'm not in the life anymore."

"You could always arrange it for free."

"For you, it'd always have been free, even back then."

"Back then" was a number of years ago, on one of Bolan's trips to Chicago. Rose got tired of her pimp beating her up and decided to go solo. He hadn't taken kindly to her decision and showed up two days later with a couple of friends to take her out of both the life and the living. Because Bolan was following up a lead that led through that particular pimp, it wasn't Rose who ended up in the morgue.

Rose had been grateful. She had also been well-informed, and finally she had agreed to talk. What she said would have put her in even more danger, except that there weren't many survivors of the Bolan blitz among the pimp's friends and patrons.

"Thanks, but I wasn't thinking of that."

Rose looked up and down at Bolan's lean, muscled height and sighed. "A man like you ought to be thinking of that. Well," she went on, "you want something. Okay. You reckon I still owe you for stomping on Pino and his buddies?"

"Maybe a little."

"How much is a little?"

"Hide somebody for twenty-four hours, until I can talk to him. Then pass him on to some friends."

"Government-type friends?"

"I thought you were straight?"

"I'm as straight as I can be. But you try runnin' a bar sometime without breakin' laws."

"No bet, Rose. These aren't that kind of government. They're not looking at the revenue stamps on your bourbon."

"Okay, then you tell me how to recognize Mr. Somebody and your friends, and it's a deal. Anything else?"

"Anybody around here running a little business?"

"Like what kind of business?"

"Crack, child porno, protection..."

"Well, there's a little porno action going on a ways north." Rose didn't quite meet his eyes. "I did one flick for him, before I went straight. Good bread, too."

"Just one?"

"Just one, and we were all grown-ups in it. But that was a while back. The guy who run things back then, he sold out to a friend. It's street talk that the guy got his money from the Vitellis."

Bolan pretended surprise. The less Rose knew about the details of his mission, the less she could be forced to tell. If the Vitellis were still in business, they'd have people who could force information out of a slab of granite.

"So they're back in business?"

"A bunch of the old hardmen and the old *consiglière*'s son, at least. You got some unfinished business with them, Milo?"

"You might say that. You might also tell me where to find where the friend hangs out."

Rose gave him an address. "I don't know for certain sure he's into kiddie porn," she added. "But he was such a scuzzball, I'd bet my ass on it."

Bolan looked the woman up and down. "That's a pretty big bet, Rose."

"Why, you—" Then she laughed. "Okay. Now how'm I to tell your friend from, say, a Vitelli goon?"

"He's about nineteen...."

WILLY LOPEZ STOOD ON THE El platform and shivered. It was a cool night for spring, and the fog was blowing in off the lake.

That wasn't the only thing making him shiver. They'd promised he was going to be safe once he'd told everything he knew about the Playa Roja, about the drugs and the new deal Gurrola was putting together. Sure he'd be safe—in the Chicago River, a floater they'd pick up some time in June, if anybody learned he'd been talking.

Maybe he'd be safe once he got out of Chicago. And he ought to make it, if he got all the way to Fort Benning. The Army didn't have people on Don Hector's payroll.

Did it?

Lopez shivered again. There was also the Witness Protection Program, but some people wound up dying real slow because the program didn't protect them.

But those were people who informed on the real syndicate, the big boys. Gurrola wasn't that big yet.

Was he?

Lopez zipped up his jacket and looked around. The platform was almost deserted except for a couple of black kids hanging out and a drunk. The drunk was walking, or more like stumbling in circles, at the end of the platform.

No train was in sight, but nobody odd in sight, either. Lopez put his hands in his pockets. The trains didn't run often this late, but they did run. Once he was on one, he'd be on his way out to Oak Park.

That wasn't where he'd expected to go, but it was what the voice on the phone had instructed, and the voice also had the right words. Even if he was walking into a trap, it beat sitting around in the middle of one. Any place Gurrola could get to him was a trap, and maybe Oak Park would surprise the man as much as it did him.

The drunk's circles were getting bigger. Lopez didn't want to get involved with the guy, but he was getting worried. Suppose the guy fell off the platform onto the third rail while he was just standing with his hands in his pockets?

Yeah, that would be a real bummer. The police would be on his tail, and they'd tell everybody where he was. Maybe if the Feds weren't a fairy tale, they'd still come and get him before Gurrola did, but it took only one cop on the take...

The drunk was weaving closer to the edge of the platform. A light glowed way off down the tracks. The train was coming.

The youth turned. He'd keep the guy from falling in front of the train. After that, Lopez was going to be on the train to Oak Park, and the wino would have to look out for himself.

EACH TIME HIS WAVERING circle brought him into the right position, Jimmy Vennera looked toward Willy Lopez. After the fourth time, he decided that Lopez wasn't keeping any kind of a lookout. Either that, or his drunk act was working even better than usual.

Well, the kid had a lot on his mind, which wasn't going to be a problem for him much longer. There was no danger that Lopez would get an ulcer. No danger at all.

Lopez's sudden move toward Vennera nearly spoiled things in spite of the hit man's careful planning. The youth had an arm out, and Vennera almost went into action on the spot. Then he saw that the kid's hand was empty. He was only trying to help a poor old drunk. Perfect.

Vennera staggered so convincingly that he nearly lost his balance. The kid gripped him by the collar, pulling him upright, pulling him close. The roar of the train grew, and its headlight hit the platform.

The silenced .22 would take too long to draw. The hit man's hand darted into the other pocket of his jacket. As Lopez pulled him closer, Vennera rammed the ice pick up under the kid's jaw and into his brain. He yanked the ice pick free with one hand, and with the other pushed hard. The youth was dead, but his punctured brain hadn't got the message to his arms and legs. They flailed wildly, carrying him to the edge of the platform and over.

Vennera heard people shouting, brakes hissing and the scream of steel wheels on steel tracks. He heard something else, too—the sizzle of a body hitting the charged third rail. And smelled something.

Because of the train and the third rail, nobody would look for any other cause of death. Lopez would be a mess.

It was too bad that the kid had been dead when he hit the rail. Otherwise he might have felt something while it fried him. But Vennera was a realist. He knew you couldn't win them all.

6

The house was an unprepossessing structure surrounded by a five-foot wall that was topped by strands of barbed wire. The guards at the front gate sat watching a fourteen-inch television, unconcerned with any potential breaches of security. They probably thought that anybody who actually tried to get in through the gate would be legitimate.

Bolan decided that their death certificate might read, Guessed Wrong.

Of course, that depended on what he did and what was going on inside the house. If nothing criminal was taking place, the people inside would survive the night.

If it came to shooting, though, Bolan had a message he wanted to send. He pulled on a ski mask, the same kind and color worn by the man who had hit Ramon Villegas. It wouldn't take much for the Vitellis and their allies to decide that Ramon Villegas's enemies—call them the Gurrola mob—were after them, too.

Bolan made a complete circuit of the wall. The rear entrance was a driveway with a locked gate, and no guards on duty at the actual entrance. A quick look revealed four guards lounging among the cars parked at the rear of the house. Three of the assembled vehicles were limousines owned by people with more money than taste.

Legal or not, it looked as if the house were having a busy night. There was nothing more Bolan could learn from the outside. Time for the penetration.

He returned to the front of the house and found a shadowed place by one corner. He pulled two packages of hamburger loaded with sleeping pills out of his jacket pockets. The old trick should get things off on the right foot, as long as the dogs weren't trained to take food only from their handler.

They weren't. The barking got louder as the dogs discovered the hamburger, without making the guards move. Then the barking faded. In five minutes everything was quiet inside the walls.

By that time the guards were suspicious. One of them went inside, leaving the other standing in front of the open gate. This gave Bolan his chance.

He slipped along the wall, silent as a cat and deadly as a stalking tiger until the last five yards. Then a twig snapped under Bolan's foot, and the guard jumped, drew a pistol and started looking around.

He didn't look in Bolan's direction until the warrior had covered four of those last five yards. It was too late. Bolan exploded out of the shadows and drove a stiffened hand into the guard's solar plexus.

The man doubled up, trying to breathe, scream and vomit all at the same time. After a few seconds he gave up trying to do any of them and simply collapsed.

As he did, Bolan heard footsteps on the walk inside and saw the gate swinging shut. He lunged for it, but the electric motor was too powerful. A moment later the gate clicked shut, leaving Bolan outside and the other guard inside.

Fortunately for Bolan, the guard had one of the dogs over one arm and the remote-control transmitter for the gate in the other. He also spent two seconds within Bolan's reach.

Against the Executioner, that was far too long. This time the stiffened hand struck the man's throat. He toppled backward, the dog landing on top of him, the transmitter landing with a crack on the sidewalk.

Bolan could have blown the lock on the gate, but he was ready to gamble that the guards hadn't given the alarm yet.

Bolan scrambled up the nearest tree that reached to the top of the wall and pulled out a pair of insulated wire-cutters. They made short work of the wire. He dropped down into the shadows behind a huge beech tree, pocketed the cutters, then studied the grounds.

The security system inside the wall included lights on the house and probably TV monitors, but no lights on the wall. This left patches of shadow that gave Bolan a slow but secure route to the house.

So far things were going his way, but he'd begun to wonder what was up ahead. People who ran chicken houses usually had better security than this. Was everybody so busy watching or playing that they weren't monitoring the TV screens? Or had those limos brought so many soldiers that the men inside thought they could handle anybody who *did* make it into the house?

Guessing was a waste of time, and time was something Bolan never wasted once he'd committed himself to a probe or assault. Once he'd worked his way to the house, he began a low crawl along the wall. The bushes provided plenty of cover, and trees and vines offered a choice of half a dozen ways onto the roof.

Bolan picked a vine supported by a peeling red trellis and began to climb. As he rolled onto the roof, the house security finally began to wake up. Outdoor lights started to rotate, illuminating the grounds. Two men trotted out the front door, one of them carrying a radio and both carrying Uzis.

The warrior wormed his way across the roof tiles. In the middle of the house was an atrium with a skylight. The glass of the skylight had been painted black on the inside. Bolan pulled out a glass cutter and began to scribe a peephole in one corner.

As he cut, he listened for any noise from the security team. They were still quiet. Either they hadn't found the men Bolan had taken out, or they were trying to make him believe they hadn't. The second would be more professional; Bolan decided to assume that.

A suction cup held the circle of glass in place while Bolan scribed the last couple of inches. He lifted it clear and peered through the hole.

He'd chosen the right spot. He had a clear view of the atrium and everybody and everything in it.

The new *consiglière* of the Vitelli Family and four of his soldiers were sitting on benches by the atrium pool. Two of the men carried Uzis, and the jackets of the others showed the bulges of shoulder holsters.

That was pretty hefty opposition for one man, even not counting the guards outside and others who might be elsewhere in the house. Bolan still had to force himself not to just dive through the skylight and start shooting.

The soldiers were watching a naked fat man, who matched the description of the new owner, approach a young girl lying facedown on a lounge chair. She was bound and gagged to keep her from screaming.

In the near-silence he could hear high-pitched sobbing and an occasional sigh or groan from elsewhere in the house. He didn't know about guards or customers, but that girl wasn't the only one who might need help.

Bolan could solve the tactical problems of being a one-man army in his sleep, and now he was wide awake, every sense stretched to full alert. First step: diversions front and back to get the enemy soldiers moving away from where he would strike, and moving away from the children.

The Executioner found a position on the roof where he could see both the front and rear of the house. The guards in front had found the men at the gate and were bending over them. They might be giving the alarm, but they weren't alert themselves.

That lack of alertness killed them—along with two rounds of the Desert Eagle.

He heard shouts and scraping furniture from below. The shots from the big .44 must have sounded like the wrath of God, which was actually fairly close to what was going to hit the men below.

Bolan armed a concussion grenade and heaved it out into the parking lot. Guards staggered and windows shattered. A flash-bang grenade followed, sailing through a broken windshield and blowing out the car's remaining windows. A screaming guard clapped his hands over his eyes blinded by flying glass.

Then the warrior threw two incendiary grenades. One landed on a BMW's front seat. The other rolled straight under a Cadillac limousine. Phosphorous flared white, then its blaze was lost in the glare of a gas tank exploding.

The Executioner crashed through the skylight, hit the floor, rolled and came up with the Beretta in one hand and the Desert Eagle in the other.

The Beretta was enough for the hardman with the M-16. A 3-round burst punched the guy to the floor, his trigger finger setting off several aimless rounds before his brain got the message that he was dead.

The next man to face the Executioner was the owner. He held the girl across his chest with one hand and held up a video camera with the other. He must have thought that his human shield protected all his vital spots. He'd forgotten his head and the camera he was holding in front of it.

Two Magnum rounds drove through the camera from lens to grip, smashing it back into the man's face. He screamed in pain, and dropped both the camera and the girl.

The Executioner grabbed the girl and half pushed, half threw her into the kitchen, out of the line of fire.

The *consiglière* suddenly loomed up behind the fat man. Two more rounds from the huge .44 took him out of play. Bolan gambled on none of the other children being out of their rooms. He armed two fragmentation grenades and heaved them down the hall. The skylight caved in, the shattering glass almost drowning out the screams. Before the last bits of glass hit the floor, Bolan was leaping over the dead *consiglière*, the Beretta poised at his hip.

Hardly anyone in the atrium had survived the blasts.

"The house is going to burn," the warrior shouted. "Get out while you can!" It was possible that there was somebody left in this place, besides the children, who didn't deserve to burn alive.

A half-naked man appeared, clutching a young girl. He was shaking like a tree in a high wind and couldn't take his eyes off the muzzle of the Desert Eagle as it swung his way.

"I'm not—I didn't—I just came here for—"

"Well, you won't be coming here again. Not you, not anybody else. Out!"

The man took two steps, then the girl bit him on the hand. He yelled an obscenity, dropped her and raised a fist. She dodged the punch and fell into the pool.

Before Bolan could spare a thought for the man, shots from the hall cut through the smoke, narrowly missing Bolan but not missing the man at all. With a hole in his thigh, another in the side of his head, he toppled into the pool.

The warrior dived for any cover the room offered, not expecting much and wondering if the next shots might be the last he'd ever hear. Instead, he heard the stutter of an Ingram, and a Vitelli hardman reeled out of the hall, his chest ruined by .45 slugs.

As the man joined the other bodies littering the floor, Bolan glimpsed someone scurrying away down the hall. From the back it was hard to be sure, but the man certainly had Fredo Guzman's thick-necked, broad-shouldered build.

Bolan decided to gamble on the man being Guzman and in a position to guard the Executioner's rear. He was going to have to search the house, or else leave children to burn.

It wasn't a long search, thanks to two of the older children. They gathered up their fellow inmates of Hell and were bringing them downstairs.

"Is that everybody?" Bolan asked when he reached them.

"All of us, anyway," the girl replied.

"I'm not worried about anybody but you kids. Now let's get moving, because I don't think all the people who kept you here are dead."

They weren't, as Bolan discovered the minute he reached the kitchen. A burst from an Uzi shattered the windows the moment the gunner detected movement. Then a Mace cannister came flying after the bullets.

Bolan heard the sound of a high-powered engine revving up. Then, with a crash of splintering wood and splitting brick, one of the limousines rammed the door. Bolan saw the door fly apart, the windshield star and crack and Fredo Guzman at the wheel.

The warrior vaulted onto the hood, then down onto the ground. He jerked the driver's door open with one hand and rabbit-punched Guzman with the other. He didn't pull the punch, either. Guzman had to not only look hurt but *be* hurt, or his cover would be blown.

The undercover cop sprawled on the pavement as Bolan grabbed the children and pushed them into the limousine. Bullets sang through the air around him but hit nothing except the limousine, which was armored.

When all seven children were packed into the vehicle, Bolan threw it into reverse. Once he knew he wasn't going to run over Guzman, he cut the wheel hard to the right.

The parking lot and driveway were a roadblock of disabled or burning cars, providing cover to the last few soldiers.

He swung around the house, splintered a stand of privet hedge and aimed the limousine for the front gate. The gate was still closed, and a hardman was standing in front of it with a raised automatic.

"Heads down!" Bolan shouted, and floored the gas pedal. The guard managed one shot before the limousine's fender clipped him and spun him away.

With half the gate decorating the front of the limousine like an oversize hood ornament, Bolan swung left. He knew the route to the nearest hospital, and he was going to get the kids close to it before he ditched the car.

He thought he saw blue police lights flashing as he finished the turn. Just to be safe he cut through an alley, slowing only a bit, then accelerated again as he returned to the streets.

Nobody in the limousine needed the police. The children needed doctors and no hassle for a few days. Bolan needed to get on with the mission.

IT TOOK THREE TRIES FOR Cesare Vitelli to get through to Danny Lipardo. This was partly due to its being three o'clock in the morning. It was also due to Lipardo's being pleasantly occupied with the maid.

Even after Vitelli got through, it took some time to turn a shouting match into communication. Vitelli finally admitted that there was nothing to link that night's massacre with Gurrola's people except the killer's ski mask.

"Then I'm as eager as you to find and destroy this man," Lipardo said. "Describe him."

"I tell you, he wore the dark red—"

"I know." Lipardo bit back the "you fool." He had to keep some sort of peace with Vitelli if they were to have any hope of solving this mystery. "But was he tall or short? Fat or thin?"

"Tall, over six feet, moved like an athlete."

Relief swept Lipardo. The only one of his soldiers unaccounted for was Vennera, and he couldn't look six feet tall on stilts.

"I tell you two things, Cesare. One is that neither I nor Don Hector would do such a thing to our friends, or let any of our soldiers do it.

"The other, and this I swear by my mother's honor, is that if one of ours did this without orders, I'll find him. Then what's left of him afterward, I'll give to you."

"You swear this?"

Vitelli seemed to have an old-fashioned belief in formidable oaths. He made Lipardo swear quite a few before he decided to be satisfied.

"Do you need men?" Lipardo asked. As a gesture, this cost nothing. If the Vitellis really needed soldiers, on the other hand, and the Langas men were now too few for their job at the Playa Roja—

"We defend our own."

"Then good luck and good hunting."

THE EXECUTIONER HAD no trouble reaching Hal Brognola. The Justice Department man sounded as if he'd been sleeping within arm's reach of the telephone.

The line was secure, but it was nearly dawn, Bolan was tired and the gory details of the night's work could wait. He summarized the job and concluded, "When I saw the blue lights were hanging in there on my tail, I took a shortcut through a park. That left me a just a couple of blocks from the hospital. None of the kids were injured during the hit, so I could bail out with a clear conscience. If the police didn't pick them up, one of the older ones would have hiked into the emergency room."

"Nice work," Brognola said. "But something not so nice also happened last night. Our would-be informant from the Playa Roja fell off an El platform."

"Or was pushed?"

"That, too."

Bolan frowned. Before he could say anything, Brognola continued. "Don't worry about Rose. We'll have her guarded or getting away."

"Better make it guarded. I don't think she wants to pull up stakes and start over again at her age."

"You sound pretty sure of that."

"A lot of experience made me an expert on people like Rose."

"I'm not arguing. Just reminding you that *my* decisions have to go through channels."

"Then start them going. I've got a call to make. If the Playa Roja isn't coming to us, then I've got to go to the Playa Roja."

7

When Danny Lipardo finished describing the hit on the chicken ranch, there was a long silence on the telephone line before Hector Gurrola replied.

"The final decision will be mine," Gurrola said finally. "But I want your advice. Should we go on as we have planned?"

"Against the Playa Roja?"

"Have you other operations in mind?"

"Not yet."

"Don't devise new ones without consulting me."

"Of course, Don Hector."

"I do suggest one thing. Find those who have been protected by the Vitellis and Langas or worked for them. Tell them how weak their protectors have become. Offer my protection, in my name, if they wish it."

Lipardo grinned. It was always a pleasure to be told to do what he had decided on anyway.

"As you wish. But I suggest we don't protect anyone who sells children. Let the six-foot bogeyman have them."

"Are you tenderhearted all at once?"

"No. It's only that so far the police have no leads on Villegas, Ignacio Luna or the Vitellis. Willy Lopez, they think is an accident. But now we move against the Playa Roja. Sooner or later, the police will find a trail. I want to make sure that it leads them nowhere."

"Wise, but what does this have to do with children and pornographers?"

"Too many of the child-buyers are stupid. They think no one will miss one child. This is true. So they go from one child to another. Sooner or later one *is* missed. Then the police come on the scene, searching. Better that they not find us when they do."

"I approve of your reasoning. I don't think our friends will be setting up that operation again soon. But if they talk of doing so, warn them.

"I'll be going as far south as I had expected," Gurrola concluded. "I'll also be gone as much as another five days. Until then, you command in my place."

"As you wish, Don Hector."

The connection broke. Lipardo briefly considered the wisdom of Gurrola's suffering an "accident" on his trip, but Lipardo had few reliable connections in Miami or Colombia.

It had also occurred to him that the man who had destroyed the chicken ranch might be the legendary Executioner. The Executioner—and he and the Bedbug were being left alone to deal with him.

They might die—Lipardo had no illusions about being immortal or invulnerable. But neither was the Executioner. They might be the ones to finally bring him down.

And then? The Mafia wouldn't pay a penny of their million-dollar reward to a rival, not even for the Executioner's head. But it wasn't only the Mafia who wanted the Executioner's head.

The man who took him down would have allies all over the world. He would become the boss, even if Hector Gurrola married all of Salvador Lirio's granddaughters.

A SMOGGY, HUMID late-spring evening was settling down over Chicago when Bolan took his rented green Pontiac off the expressway a couple of miles west of the Loop. Keeping a lookout for tails, he zigzagged toward the Playa Roja.

There were actually three Playa Rojas, each with its own manager but ultimately run by the Lirio family. The chain had been founded by Luis Martinez, an old enemy of Salvador Lirio's. Hal Brognola's Intel had said that the old man's feud with the Martinez family went back about sixty years, and might have made him careless about his choice of allies.

Certainly the money Don Salvador had used to buy the chain from the Martinez heir was laundered gang money. But their knowing this at Stony Man Farm didn't prove that Salvador Lirio knew it.

Bolan was heading for the first Playa Roja, the original converted storefront less than a mile from where Ramon Villegas had died. It was the other two Playa Rojas that got into the newspapers. One was on the lakefront north of the Loop, the other in an expensive suburb beyond O'Hare International Airport. They had plastic Mexican decor, waitresses with punk hairdos, yuppie customers and what looked like the same menu as the original Playa Roja.

Nobody who had ever eaten at the original one could be fooled by the imitations. Maybe long enough to sit down and order, but not after the first bite. Certainly not even halfway to the plastic flan that was the featured dessert in the two imitations.

Bolan parked the Pontiac two blocks from the restaurant, fed the parking meter a quarter and began drifting toward his goal. He was dark enough to blend into a Hispanic neighborhood, for all his six feet plus. It was also easy for him to imitate the casualness of someone at home in this neighborhood.

Inside, Bolan ordered coffee and a plate of the house appetizers. For that, they would let him stay long enough to study the place.

Fredo Guzman had said that Enrique Dino, the manager, would be more than happy to cooperate in return for protection. Bolan didn't doubt Guzman's judgment, but he had to set up a convincing "kidnapping" of Dino. Otherwise Lipardo's men would go after the man's family and the restaurant staff.

Guzman either hadn't realized this or didn't care. Bolan hoped it was the first. He didn't like the idea of working with a man who was casual about putting innocent people into the line of fire.

Occasionally Bolan ate a mouthful of food or sipped coffee. Most of the time his eyes roamed the room, from crowded table to crowded table, up to the old tin ceiling under its coating of greasy red paint, back down to the faded prints of fighting cocks and Mexican soldiers adorning the walls.

He was careful not to look too long at Enrique Dino. The manager kept popping in and out of the kitchen, talking to the waitresses and busboys, occasionally stopping to chat with a regular customer.

Outside, a police siren wailed, and Bolan saw the manager stiffen, try to hide it, then relax as the police car rolled past without stopping. He tried to hide that, too.

"Anything else, *señor*?"

Bolan looked up, to see a middle-aged waitress with Conchita embroidered on her dress standing by his table. He was about to say no when movement out in front caught his eye.

Two men were standing outside, wearing windbreakers and faded chinos. Like the manager, they were trying to look casual about everything. Being professionals, they were doing a much better job.

In fact, they would probably have fooled almost anyone except the man who now watched them.

Bolan finally had to order to keep up his act. He suspected that the red snapper with rice was going to be wasted, because the Langas hitters would be in action long before it arrived. The men couldn't be anything else.

The red snapper arrived, along with extra side dishes, cucumbers and fried potatoes. "Compliments of the manager," Conchita said as she put the hot plates down beside the fish.

"I'll be back to thank him personally when I'm done," Bolan replied. Score one for Enrique Dino. He'd had the sense to give Bolan an excuse for going back to the kitchen.

Now, if the soldiers outside just gave Bolan the time for that....

He actually got about halfway through the meal before his stomach warned him that any more would slow him down. The soldiers were still outside, but they hadn't moved. Maybe they were just scouting, like Bolan.

Maybe. That would be a fine coincidence. It would also mean that the warrior had to get Enrique Dino out of here tonight because the next soldiers the drug lords sent to the Playa Roja wouldn't be scouts.

Bolan looked toward the kitchen door, where Enrique Dino was standing. When he noticed Bolan looking his way, his head jerked.

Then it jerked again, drawn toward the front of the restaurant. Dino's eyes widened. Bolan shifted his own gaze so that his peripheral vision let him track both the manager and movement at the front door.

The Beretta rode in a shoulder holster under a tweed sports jacket. Bolan drew the 93-R as Dino turned back into the kitchen, nearly colliding with a busboy.

The warrior kept the drawn Beretta beneath table level and watched the two soldiers pull on ski masks. Then they pushed their way through the revolving door. One of them dashed for the kitchen. The other stopped just inside the door, surveyed the room and made a hand signal to Bolan.

The man's other hand held a Browning Hi-Power.

Bolan waited long enough for the man's eyes to focus on his own visible left hand, looking for a recognition signal. The man also waited a moment, until he saw that the recognition signal wasn't coming, then swung his Browning toward Bolan.

The Executioner shot the man in the chest, sending a single 9 mm slug between two occupied tables. The man jerked up the Browning and fired a round into the ceiling. It shorted the wiring of a ceiling fan, and the electrical arc sizzled as loud as the gunshot.

Bolan didn't wait for the man to fall. He tipped over his own table, dumping the remains of his dinner all over his neighbors and ducked behind it. The table was old-fashioned heavy wood, a solid shield.

The neighbors screamed and swore as sauce and fish dripped from their clothing. Bolan didn't have time to apologize. He'd do his best not to get them shot. The cleaning bills were their problem.

He looked for the second hitter and Enrique Dino, who had to be the man's target. The kitchen had swallowed them both.

Two shots roared from the kitchen, and at the same time, the revolving door started to whirl.

Bolan saw two more soldiers trying to get in at the same time as half the people in the restaurant tried to get out. Instead of taking down the soldiers, the warrior's job had suddenly become preventing innocent people from being crushed or trampled to death.

"Down on the floor!" he shouted. He grabbed a chair, swung it back and forth to build up speed, then heaved it through the front window.

Fifty square feet of plate glass dissolved with a crash that drowned out screams that came from the kitchen. The gaping frame gave the mob of diners another exit—and the soldiers outside another entrance. Bolan saw them appear beyond the jagged remnants of the window. He knew that they didn't have any scruples about shooting into crowds.

The Desert Eagle leaped into his hand and roared. The last bits of glass shivered out of the frame, and one of the soldiers flew backward. The .44 slug punched into his jaw and out the back of his skull.

The other man at least had the nerve to draw, but his first shot was a clean miss, and he didn't get a second. His .44 hit was a gut shot. He went down folded double and screaming.

Bolan whirled in a low crouch, leaving crowd control to luck and any cool heads among his fellow diners. He'd turned his back on the kitchen, which still held at least one live enemy, and by rights he ought be dead.

A masked man was lying on the floor in front of the men's room. His chest was a bloody mess, and there was more blood on the floor under him.

The Executioner elbowed his way through the crowd hurrying toward the safety of the street. Enrique Dino was huddled in a corner, as pale as flour and looking ready to have a heart attack on the spot. A 9 mm Star automatic hung from one limp hand.

The warrior twisted the Star out of the man's hand, shoved it into his own belt, then jerked Dino to his feet.

"What—"

"Shut up!" Bolan snarled in Spanish. Then he shouted, "Come on! Help me with this son of a bitch! If the boss can ask him a few questions—"

The idea of currying favor with Gurrola was irresistibly tempting to the men out in back. They came through the back door with their guns drawn but low. All their attention shifted to Dino, and they grinned.

They were still grinning when Bolan shot both of them. One of them got his gun up before collapsing.

The kitchen staff seized the opportunity to flee the scene.

Bolan stepped over the dead hardmen, dragging Dino with him.

"Who—" the manager gasped.

"Quiet." Bolan kicked open the back door, looked both ways along the alley, then ripped out the telephone. This was another situation where the police meant confusion and security leaks, not help.

The Executioner prodded Dino in the back with the muzzle of the .44. The manager nearly fell down his own back stairs and barely caught himself on a trashbin. The rusty, jagged edge of the lid gouged his hand.

Bolan handed the man a handkerchief. As Dino started binding the cut, a car swung into the alley—a light blue Chevrolet with two men in the front seat.

Bolan switched weapons. Now the Beretta jabbed Dino in the back, and the Desert Eagle rode ready for action in Bolan's right hand.

The car pulled up in front of Bolan. The driver rolled down his window and smiled. "Got—"

"*¡Hoy!*" his companion shouted, and started to raise his weapon.

Bolan shot the more alert and therefore more dangerous man in the head. The muzzle blast of Big Thunder half stunned the driver, so Bolan didn't bother shooting him. He merely grabbed the man by the arm and jerked.

The hitter flew out of the vehicle and crashed headfirst into the trashbin. When he landed facedown in the filth of the alley, his head was at an impossible angle to his shoulders.

"Get in," Bolan ordered. Now both pistols were aimed at Enrique Dino.

The manager looked as if he couldn't make up his mind—obey this gun-toting apparition and die later, or have a heart attack and die now.

Finally he obeyed Bolan. He even found the strength to push the dead hardman out of the passenger seat. By then Bolan was strapped in.

"Where are you talking me?" Dino asked as Bolan put the car in gear.

Bolan burned rubber coming out of the alley and cut right. "To a safe place."

"The grave is a safe place," Dino replied.

"If that's the kind of safety you want, I can always take you back." Bolan swung onto Seventeenth Street.

"No. No, I—I'll come quietly."

Bolan gave him a brief nod, then settled down to finding a circuitous route back to his Pontiac.

8

Enrique Dino kept up with Bolan better than the warrior expected. He also had some street smarts. When they came within sight of the Pontiac, he stayed under cover as Bolan moved toward the vehicle.

No blast of lead greeted the Executioner. The warning of danger came more subtly. The hood wasn't latched the way it had been, and Bolan saw chipped spots in its paint.

He backed away from the car, into the shadows of the alley where Dino waited.

"Somebody's made us. The car's been tampered with."

"A bomb?"

"Probably."

A stick of dynamite could be wired into a car's ignition system in a minute by a good man. Gurrola and Lipardo would certainly have men good enough.

"Shit." Dino put a whole world of disgust into that one word.

Bolan nodded. "We'd better move out on foot."

"Where to?"

"You'll find out when we get there."

"But if we get separated, how will I know where to go?"

Bolan looked the manager up and down. The question made sense, but the secret of the safehouse wasn't his to give.

"Let's try not to get separated."

Bolan thought of adding that if they did, it wouldn't matter if Dino didn't know where to go. Unless Bolan had completely wiped out the hardmen in the area, Dino would have only one destination—an anonymous grave.

Bolan saw that fact dawning in Dino's eyes. Before he could say anything, a teenage boy darted from behind a trash bin. He crouched by the Pontiac, working on the lock with professional skill. He had the door open before even Bolan's trained eye recognized him as a thief.

The warrior opened his mouth to shout a warning, but the boy must have hot-wired the Pontiac the moment he reached the ignition. The explosion drowned out Bolan's words.

The blast wasn't big enough for dynamite. Probably a grenade, the Executioner thought, or a chunk of plastic explosive. It still wrecked both the car and the would-be car thief. Dino gaped at the blood spattered over the shattered windshield, then cringed as gasoline from the ruptured tank ignited.

Bolan's attention was elsewhere. Two men—no, four, because the two had another pair covering them—were walking toward the shattered vehicle. Bolan shoved a fresh magazine into the Desert Eagle. He'd already reloaded the Beretta, but the .44 had the extra range he'd need for the second pair.

The men in the lead were alert. Something about the body in the front seat warned them that it wasn't their intended victim. They reacted like professionals, drawing and going to cover at the same time.

Bolan lowered the Desert Eagle, then felt his arm being grabbed. He turned to glare at Dino.

"Why didn't you shoot?"

"They know they didn't get the right men, but they don't know who they did get. They also don't know that we're still around. Shooting would have told them that."

"I see."

"Good. Use your eyes and ears from now on, and not your mouth. And don't *ever* grab my arm."

Dino opened his mouth, then settled for a nod. The man wasn't an innocent, Bolan knew, but he was no master criminal. He also wasn't a complete fool.

Probably the best punishment for him after he talked would be to send a copy of his confession to his wife. From what Guzman said, she was a first-class shrew.

The four hardmen down the street were also first-class. It was a full minute before Bolan noticed that the covering pair were gone. Where, he didn't know, but with them on the move and himself fixed, they had suddenly acquired an edge.

Without Dino it would be easy enough to take the edge back. With him, changing from hunted to hunter was going to be hard, maybe impossible.

Bolan motioned Dino toward the rear of the alley. He saw the manager backing away, then drew the Beretta. Two 9 mm rounds slammed into the burning car. They only punched out the last bits of glass in a window, but that was enough.

A shout in Spanish rose from an airway. Somebody was giving or maybe asking a recognition code. He was also revealing his location. The two primary hardmen were good, but not perfect. They didn't realize that somebody firing on the wrecked car might not be a friend making a mistake.

Now, if it would take them a minute or two to realize their mistake...

Bolan slapped Dino on the back. "That produce store with the yellow awning. Run!"

The manager ran ponderously but somehow crossed the fifty yards to the store fast enough. Bolan heard another shout, this one angry, before he followed Dino.

Two police cars raced past, sirens screaming and blue lights flashing. They careered around the corner and vanished. Bolan realized that he'd been hearing police sirens for quite a while, but had tuned them out during the first confrontation.

He couldn't go on doing that. The Playa Roja would be swarming with policemen before the night was over, and sooner, rather than later, they'd know that Enrique Dino was missing.

Then they'd be determined to find him. Bolan had to prevent that, because if the police took Enrique Dino alive, he wouldn't stay that way very long. An informant was a sitting duck in Cook County Jail. Gurrola might even be able to break Dino out. Then the whole battle at the Playa Roja would have been a waste.

Bolan looked up and down the deserted street. From open windows he could hear mariachi music, but not even much of that. This was a weekday night; people had to go to work or school in the morning. Even those who didn't, weren't going to sit out on their front steps with police sirens wailing through the neighborhood.

"Look out for anything suspicious," Bolan warned. He started to pick the padlock on the security screen across the door.

The manager was curious, but he'd had his lesson. He'd just reported a police car stopping two men when Bolan opened the lock.

"Come on. Out the back, then up to the roof."

They slipped through musty darkness that smelled of old vegetables and overripe fruit, then out the back door. The back stairs were cleaner than the store, and brightly lighted. Nobody inside the apartments seemed awake, though.

Crouching below the level of back windows, Bolan and Dino climbed to the roof. From behind a chimney, Bolan watched the police car drive off.

Good. The police weren't on their trail, but they were in the neighborhood. That might keep the hardmen looking in too many directions at once to focus on Bolan and Dino.

A series of roofs studded with skylights and ventilators stretched three-quarters of a block south. At the far end was the El. If they reached it and walked along the tracks to the nearest station, they'd be arriving from an unexpected direction.

They scrambled along the roofs toward the El. In places there was a fall or rise of half a story that Bolan maneuvered easily. Dino needed help. By the time they approached the tracks, the manager's clothes were black, and he was gasping like a fish out of water. He didn't even have breath to ask what they were going to do when they reached the El tracks.

Bolan had to lower Dino onto the service walkway beside the tracks when they finally reached them. The manager staggered, nearly toppled off onto the charged third rail, then gripped the railing. He'd almost caught his breath by the time Bolan swung down beside him.

"And now?"

"A little walk, then a ride on the El."

They started walking west, between the tracks. Bolan remembered that if two trains passed each other, the space between wasn't wide enough for a man. But if they met one train before they reached the station, it would surprise him.

A train was just pulling out in the opposite direction as they approached the station. If any passengers were looking out from the rear car, they didn't see two rumpled figures walking up the tracks toward the platform.

Somebody was watching the tracks, though, somebody who knew what he was looking for and what to do about it when he saw it.

Only alertness and speed saved the Executioner and his charge. The man in the black plastic raincoat had drawn before Bolan recognized one of the hit men who'd approached his car. His response was simple snap-shooting, a 3-round burst from the Beretta.

The man disappeared, but two shots told Bolan that he was still in action. Bolan and Dino also went to ground behind a pile of ties.

Not good. The gang boss had guarded the top of the station stairs. At the bottom would be another hardman. Or maybe a ticket taker, who'd already be calling the police at the sound of the shots.

No. El stations weren't usually staffed this late. A passenger paid the fare on the train. If the police would just hold off and another train come along soon enough . . .

Bolan didn't believe in answered prayers, but another train did show up about two minutes later. As it rolled toward the station, the hardman sat on the bench and opened a newspaper that probably hid his gun.

No doubt he assumed his opponents wouldn't dare shoot with the passengers around. He was right, but it hadn't occurred to him that Bolan might have other resources besides guns. Two minutes spent opening the toolboxes on the piles of tiles had given the Executioner some useful additions to his arsenal.

As the train rolled past Bolan, the brakes hissed and it slowed. He scrambled onto the rear platform of the last car, squatting below the level of the window.

A quick look around the side of the car showed the gunman getting to his feet, folding the newspaper and shifting to where he could watch anyone getting on or off. Bolan did a little shifting, too. He shifted his grip on the crowbar he'd found in one of the toolboxes.

As the train passed the hardman, Bolan swung the hooded end of the crowbar and caught the man around an ankle, yanking him off the platform. The warrior jumped down and crouched over the gunner while two passengers got off and one got on.

The one who got on didn't seem to notice that his companion who'd been waiting hadn't joined him. The hardman was unconscious, but Bolan still kept low until the train had rolled out of sight toward the Loop.

That caution paid off. Another hardman bounded up the stairs. He ran toward the end of the platform, pulling an Ingram from under the raincoat.

Bolan had to let the man get off one burst, just in case he was on the side of the law. It was a long burst, which chewed splinters from the pile of ties. That satisfied Bolan. He rose from his crouch and snapped off two shots toward the subgunner. The man toppled off the platform and hit a gap between the ties, falling all the way down to the parked cars below.

Enrique Dino crept out from behind the ties, dabbing at a bloody cheek. He stood up and walked toward the platform, looking around nervously, as if he expected the tracks to open up and swallow him at every moment.

"Come on," Bolan said. He dragged the unconscious hardman under the platform and covered him roughly with trash.

"That should confuse things a little more."

"You can't confuse me any more," Dino said. "Please. I'll tell even those things that I'm ashamed of."

"You certainly will."

"But I beg you—where are we going?"

"Out of here."

"You—"

"I can still leave you for the police or your old friends." Bolan pointed under the platform. "I'm not going to, because you had the courage to shoot one of them already tonight. That makes you worth saving, in my books. It also means you go out the hard way if they catch you."

Dino shrugged. "You call this the easy way?"

"You're alive, aren't you?"

"Very well. Upstairs or down?"

"Downstairs. I want to make a phone call."

9

The man Bolan addressed as Don Salvador sat in an armchair and held a cane across his lap. That and the snow-white hair were the only signs that he was much past sixty.

He was actually eighty-four. He'd begun as a boy, picking tomatoes in Texas before the First World War. Now he was worth close to sixty million dollars. He'd made very few mistakes while amassing this fortune. One he'd made in the recent past could undo everything he'd worked for.

That was his alliance with Hector Gurrola. He'd joined forces with the man in order to settle accounts with his old enemy, Luis Martinez. It turned out to be unnecessary, because Martinez went blind and retired, then died two years ago.

By then Gurrola had a firm grip on the good name of the Lirio family. All he had to do was squeeze, and it would be destroyed.

Salvador Lirio might have been willing to face that for himself. He and his wife had long since been citizens. They couldn't be deported. They were too rich to starve, and too old to put in jail.

But Lirio's children and grandchildren were another matter. Above all, his favorite grandchild, Angelita, la Principesa, must not be shamed.

Without the children and grandchildren, Bolan might have doubted Salvador Lirio's repentance. He might have suspected the man wasn't ashamed of his crime, only afraid of getting caught.

But it was hard to mistake Lirio's voice when he spoke of the family, particularly of Angelita. He was Bolan's ally by choice, not by fear or necessity.

The tape of Enrique Dino telling everything he knew about Gurrola played to an end, until the hiss of the recorder was the only sound in the bedroom. Don Salvador cocked his head, then smiled. He looked as if he had just finished listening to a great symphony played by an equally great orchestra and conductor.

"Beautiful," he said. "Absolutely beautiful." His English was almost completely free of any accent.

"Glad you like it," Guzman said. "Think it will do?"

"That depends on how much cooperation we find in high places," the old man replied. He held up a hand as he sensed the policeman starting to protest.

"I know. You think it will be simple when this is handed over to the men in Washington. Let me tell you, we have only just begun. All of us here." His head turned toward Bolan. "You, sir, are...?"

"My name is Milo Bruning," Bolan answered.

"Do you speak Spanish?"

"I know enough to carry on a decent conversation. I'm not sure that I speak enough to discuss serious business."

"That may not matter." Don Salvador shrugged. "I have to tell you that much of what is to be discussed tonight is *una cosa de la Raza.* You understand?"

"Perfectly," Bolan said. He knew the reluctance of many Hispanics to discuss certain matters with Anglos present. Most of it was simple self-perservation. You didn't wash your dirty linen in public, when there were people around ready to criticize you for letting it get dirty in the first place.

"Forgive me if I appear to doubt you in any way," Bolan added. "But I hope you understand that you may be in some danger. Hector Gurrola has gone too far to stop at killing you if he fears you threaten him."

"Gurrola will, I think, be a little slow on the trigger," Lirio replied. "He dreams of marrying Angelita, and it isn't mannerly to kill your bride's grandfather without very good reason."

"Even if that slows down Gurrola, there's always Danny Lipardo," Bolan pointed out. "I know I must sound repetitive, but—"

The old man smiled. "You are forgiven. I understand this quite well. But you understand, Mr. Bruning, that I'm an old gray coyote. I have been watching for hunters, traps and my own kind for more years, I suspect, than you have been alive. I'm neither frightened nor foolish. .

"And now, with all respect for your valor tonight and the hope that it will serve us well again, I must ask you to leave. I have matters to discuss with Fredo and Luna."

Bolan left without a word, annoyed at being dismissed.

WHEN DON SALVADOR FINALLY let the two policemen go, it was just before dawn. They found Bolan in the den, asleep in an old easy chair.

Or at least he was asleep until he heard the door opening. Within seconds, he was awake, the Beretta in his hand and on the move.

Guzman realized once again just how good Bolan was. If he ever did stop walking that thin line between selective and mindless destruction—well, Guzman didn't like to think of the job this would give the country's Violent Crimes officers.

Bolan holstered the Beretta and started pulling the rest of his gear together. "Are we done here?"

"Yes."

"No," Luna said. "I think we owe our friend a little more of an explanation than Don Salvador—"

"Mira!" Guzman snapped. He spoke urgently in Spanish. The language let him be angry more comfortably.

"Don Salvador takes the secrets of the people very seriously."

"He's going to have to take federal indictments as seriously if he wants to die smelling all right," Luna snapped.

"Don Salvador is old and set in his ways," Guzman replied,

"That's an explanation, not an excuse," Luna argued.

Bolan cleared his throat. "Gentlemen, I gather somebody's been holding out on me. Can I interrupt this argument to ask what? Or do I have to go back inside and ask Don Salvador?"

"I suppose we might as well come clean," Guzman said.

"Yeah," Bolan agreed. "You might as well. Seems to be a big night for that. I take it that Don Salvador has some game up his sleeve."

"Pretty much, yes," Guzman said. "He wants to handpick one of the board members of the Instituto de Fraternidad to be the first Hispanic mayor of Chicago. That means he has to stay on good terms with them all, which means not letting Anglos in on Hispanic secrets."

"It also means he doesn't have much time left," Bolan pointed out.

"Don Salvador might outlive us all, but yeah, that's true, too," Luna said.

"It's also true that Don Salvador's criminal connections would hurt more than the Lirios," Bolan added. "Which doesn't bother me, by the way. Ambition can do as much as family feeling to keep him on our side."

"Right," Guzman said. Now that the cat was out of the bag, he felt almost relieved, as though he'd got rid of a bad hangover. "But I thought you were kind of picky about the motives of your friends and allies."

"I know my own motives," Bolan replied shortly. "I hope other people know theirs, but I don't bet on it. All I ask is that I can tell the friends from the criminals before the shooting starts."

"I think you ought to know that one of the things Don Salvador hopes to do is get more city contracts for board members," Luna said. "That will give them some clout on their own, besides his fortune."

"I see. *La mordida* comes north," Bolan said. The Spanish word for "bribery" actually translated as "the bite."

Bolan knew too well just how big a bite it took out of law enforcement south of the border. And north of it, for that matter, when there was enough money floating around, as there usually was when drugs were involved.

"Much of Mexico has come north of the border, both good and bad," Guzman said.

"Tell me about it," Bolan said. "Are you really that determined to get back at us for the Mexican War?"

"If things were better in the south, you could patrol the border with two policemen and a dog," Luna stated proudly. "Do you think people would come north to a city with winters like Chicago's if they didn't have to?"

"Okay," Bolan said, holding up a hand. The two officers couldn't have paid more attention if he'd been holding a machine gun.

"Don Salvador can play all the games he wants as long as he understands the danger. I don't like seeing innocent people in danger. I can't spend all my time looking out for them and take care of Hector Gurrola as well, which is what will make everybody around here live longer and happier.

"Just keep a good eye on Enrique Dino. If this safehouse isn't, it's going to be your fault as much as the old man's. Then I'm going to think it's smarter to finish off Gurrola solo. Do we understand one another?" Bolan asked.

Both policemen nodded.

"Great. I'll be calling you in a couple of days."

10

Danny Lipardo raised the Korth Combat Magnum and emptied six rounds into the target downrange. All were head shots.

He grinned as he turned to the man known only as Snake and pulled off his ear protectors. "I'm still better than you. Pay up."

"I thought the bet wasn't settled until Jimmy—"

Lipardo punched Snake in the shoulder. "Ha! He's fine with bedroom weapons. He isn't bad with a pistol, you understand. But he's not as good as you or me."

"No."

Lipardo decided not to press for payment of the bet today. He felt too contented, as he always did after a session on the range. It was good to know that some things could still give pleasure, because the trouble at the Playa Roja certainly didn't.

They walked to the end of the range to check the targets from close up and put up new ones. None of the servants and few of the soldiers were allowed into the pistol range. They were reloading when the telephone rang.

"How goes the search for the man from the Playa Roja?" Hector Gurrola asked.

"Which man?"

"The killer, of course."

Was there an odd note in the boss's voice? Lipardo hadn't told him that the manager was missing, and Gurrola couldn't have read it in the papers. The police only said that Enrique Dino was "wanted for questioning," not that he had vanished.

If Gurrola had found out that Dino was gone and that Lipardo had concealed the fact . . .

"Or are there two men from the Playa Roja?"

Definitely there was a note in Gurrola's voice not usually heard. Lipardo was unpleasantly reminded that he didn't know all of Gurrola's sources of information.

"I wish I could say that there was only one, boss," Lipardo replied. "But the truth is, there are two. The tall killer and the manager."

At this point telling the truth was the least dangerous course. Lipardo's allies were no longer as strong as they had been a few days ago, and Gurrola might be returning with new resources. He might even be returning with someone he thought might replace Danny Lipardo.

To his relief Lipardo heard laughter on the line. "I understand why you didn't tell me sooner. You wanted to learn if Dino was alive or dead. If he was alive, you wanted to have the hunt underway."

"That's right."

"I want you to know that this doesn't anger me. I'm sure that you've done everything else as quickly and as well as any man might have." Gurrola ran down the list and sounded approving as Lipardo reported on each one.

"One thing more," he concluded.

"What is that, boss?"

"Turning the Bedbug loose on the women of the Playa Roja."

Lipardo frowned. "How many more bodies can we afford?"

"Can't he be ordered to hold back? And if he's ordered, won't he obey?"

"Yes."

Lipardo hoped he was telling the truth. These days Jimmy Vennera seemed to feel that he had a right to all the women he wanted, if he was to keep his hands off La Principesa. She had arrived today; and Lipardo recognized the look in the little man's eyes when he saw her.

"Good. If he starts ignoring orders, we have only one course of action with him."

Which was true, but that course would also deprive Lipardo of his most potent ally among Gurrola's men at a time when an unknown killer was slaughtering his allies elsewhere.

However, Vennera should see the sense of holding back with women the police might already be watching. If he didn't, then he *was* too dangerous to leave roaming about.

"Of course, boss."

"It seems that matters aren't as good as we expected, but not as bad as they could be."

"Not so bad that you must return?"

"No, but I would be returning in two days anyway. What I could do on this journey has been done. Also, remember the meeting of leaders we have planned, aboard *Sirena*. If we had to cancel that, some might say we did it out of fear. That would be foolish.''

Again Lipardo agreed with his chief. The meeting aboard the Lirio yacht was too important to cancel for anything short of all the guests being dead.

Which, Lipardo realized with a sudden chill, wasn't wholly impossible if the Executioner had taken up the fight against them.

MACK BOLAN HAD A STACK of files to work through. The warrior had to change his base, and preferably be clear of Chicago for a day or two. The solution to both problems was a quick trip back to Stony Man Farm.

Hal Brognola leaned back in his chair and watched Bolan work through the federal file on the Lirio feud with the Martinezes. Unlike some of the other files, it wasn't long.

''It looks as if whatever they were feuding about didn't get them onto the federal docket,'' Bolan said finally. He handed the folder back to Brognola.

''That doesn't mean it wasn't serious to them,'' the big Fed pointed out. ''It doesn't even mean it didn't involve federal offenses. Back then the FBI had bigger fish to fry.''

Bolan nodded. Neither he nor Brognola had been born when the feud between the two families began. J. Edgar Hoover was still dealing with Prohibition-spawned gangsters. The most advanced automatic weapon available to the criminal was a Thompson submachine gun. The total drug consumption of the whole United States was probably less than one large city's today.

To Bolan "the march of progress" sometimes looked more like a drunken stagger.

"So I don't have any reason to move against the Lirios," Bolan concluded. That ruled out a direct assault on the Lirio estate, which would almost certainly mean worse things than scandal for Salvador Lirio. Bolan couldn't risk casualties among the family, their friends, relatives and servants on the chance of getting a handful of Gurrola's soldiers or even the man himself.

Bolan picked up the next folder. "So we're back to Gurrola. Unfortunately I haven't caused him as much trouble as I'd hoped. Both the Langas and the Vitelli gangs have lost a lot of soldiers, but none of their key people except the Vitelli *consiglière*. Lipardo can apparently charm a rabid wolf when he wants to, and seems to have them sticking with him for the moment.

"So I think it's time to follow up that shortage of bomb materials I created down in Decatur. I'm going to visit Gurrola, presenting myself as a European terrorist kingpin, and see what happens."

"Any particular kind of terrorist?"

"Well, I could probably pass as Irish."

"What makes you think Gurrola cares much about European terrorism?" the Justice Department man asked.

"You said yourself that he was out of town during most of my time in Chicago, probably gone south. That means cocaine. If he makes a direct connection with the Colombians, he'll be up to his tonsils in cocaine. That's more than Chicago can handle."

Other cities offered more customers, but most of them were already somebody else's territory or even parceled out among rival drug lords. The men on the spot would fight outsiders. Some of them had more resources than Gurrola would have, even if he acquired a major slice of the Lirio fortune.

Gurrola wasn't a fool. He wouldn't pick that sort of fight. Instead, he'd move into unoccupied territory. Europe was that, as far as cocaine went. The market was there, and the Continent was developing its own drug lords, but so far there was plenty of room for new suppliers.

There also wasn't a terrorist group around that didn't need money. A big piece of the cocaine market would give them that money—and they would certainly listen to anyone who offered to help them with their supply of the drug.

Brognola nodded when Bolan ran this line of reasoning past him. "Gurrola's certainly smart enough to see the opportunity. Even if he wasn't, I'd bet on Lipardo's seeing it. If you ever have only one bullet and a chance at both Gurrola and Lipardo, consider taking out Lipardo."

Bolan made mental notes. If Lipardo was dead, then Gurrola's death would leave the gang with no one to take over except Vennera. He was too crazy for most of the other soldiers to follow him.

"I'll get the Weatherby out of hock. Oh, one more thing, Hal," Bolan added as he stood up. "Can somebody sit on Fredo Guzman for a couple of weeks?"

"Not without tipping off the Chicago Police Department that we're involved," Brognola replied. "Believe me, I've looked at his file...."

"You haven't had to deal with him."

"Striker, you have my sincere sympathy, but facts are facts. The security problem would be impossible."

Bolan frowned. So Fredo Guzman was a loose cannon that was going to have to stay loose? Probably. No big-city police department was leakproof when somebody like Gurrola was buying information. Not to mention that the shootouts would already have both police and criminals suspicious.

But Bolan needed surprise on his side. He was planning to walk into a trap and shoot the trappers before they realized who they'd caught. Even with surprise, that would be a ridiculous plan.

Or it would be for somebody who hadn't already done it at least a dozen times.

"HELLO, JIMMY," THE WAITRESS said. She peered through the crack, the door still on its chain.

Vennera noted that the chain was old and corroded. If he had to get into Conchita's apartment, the chain wouldn't stop him.

But it would make noise, and right now he didn't want noise. This wasn't the sort of building where people called the police at a few screams, but if the screams went on long enough...

"What's the matter, Conchita?" Vennera asked, managing to look hurt. "Don't you trust me?"

"You alone?"

"Would I bring other men to share even the sight of such a rose?" He knew the flattery was so outrageous that she wouldn't take it seriously, which was the way he wanted it.

"Just a minute. Let me clean away the dishes."

It took more than a minute, and Vennera suspected she was doing more than cleaning away the dishes. He listened to her footsteps coming and going rapidly, once disappearing down the hall.

He also fingered the ice pick and knife in his jacket pocket and made sure the snub-nosed Colt was ready for a quick draw from his shoulder holster. The thought of the tall man coming up the stairs and finding him standing outside Conchita's door wasn't a pleasant one. He'd be a naked target. He didn't even want any of her neighbors to get a good look at him, just in case. . . .

The door opened, and Conchita stood in the doorway, wearing a bright pink dressing gown. The color was all right, but it didn't flatter her figure.

"Sorry about the bathrobe. I spilled something on my dress and had to take it off." She smiled what was no doubt intended to be a seductive smile. "Saves you the trouble, no?"

"Undressing a fine woman is never trouble." She was so eager, it was almost pathetic.

They sat on the sofa. Conchita promptly put an arm around him. He let it rest across his shoulders, but stopped her hand when it started to grope him. He didn't want her to find out that he was armed until she was too aroused to think what it might mean.

"Easy, honey," he said. "We have all night, and I'm not made of stone."

"You'll stay?"

"Until I'm thrown out. Do you have anything to drink? Beer, if nothing else."

"Of course." She bounced up, making her heavy breasts sway under the robe. The silly creature had so few chances at a man that she was willing to make a fool of herself when one did appear.

She came back with two Coronas. "From the Playa Roja," she said. "Most of the time they don't let us take things home. But now, with the manager gone and everybody scared... Well, they don't watch so closely."

"What are they scared of?" he asked, drawing his knife to flick the bottles open.

"Everything. We don't know if the man who sent the killers will send more. We don't know what happened to Enrique Dino."

"Probably just went in his pants and ran away."

"Who knows? He could be as dead as the ones who came. The big man who killed them went away with him—this we know. I wouldn't go with such a one if I wanted to stay alive, I tell you."

This was the first Vennera had heard of the tall man taking Dino away. He wanted to grin. Maybe he wouldn't rid the world of Conchita after all, or if he did, it would be quickly.

"Where did they go?" He realized he'd sounded too eager when Conchita frowned.

"Into the night. I tell you, Jimmy, if I didn't think you were an honest man, I'd wonder about your asking."

He shrugged. "If it bothers you to talk about it..."

"No. It's doesn't bother me. You're too nice. But the police said that if anyone came asking about the manager or the tall man, we should tell them."

"Conchita!" Vennera cupped the woman's round face in both hands. "You wouldn't do such a thing to me!"

"What have you to fear?"

"I have to fear that the police think any Mexican is a criminal or an illegal. Have you never had that trouble?"

"True. Well, I'll be very nice about this, and say nothing. Only please, Jimmy, I want you to be nice to me."

There was only one form of niceness she wanted. Fortunately it was a kind that Vennera had never failed to deliver yet. They were both sweating when they finished the first time, sweating harder the second time.

When he reached for her a third time, she slapped his hand aside. "Oh, Jimmy. Not again, not now."

"You promised—"

"That you could stay the night. Well, you can. You kept your promise, so I keep mine. But no more, not now."

The blood began to sing in Vennera's ears as she reached for the robe. "I won't beg."

"I wasn't asking you to."

"No, I'm a man, and a man *takes*."

Her eyes widened at his tone. Before she could move anything else, the knife was in his hand. It sang through the air, pinning the sleeve of her robe to the arm of the sofa.

Too surprised to scream, she tried instead to pull her sleeve free. Vennera slapped one hand over her mouth and whipped the knife free with the other.

"On your knees, whore, and be quiet!"

She went on her knees, but looked back at him with terror-struck eyes.

He wielded the knife deftly, and several minutes later he had the address in Rockford of a house where people from all three Playa Rojas had gone when they needed to hide for a while. That was more than he had known an hour ago, certainly.

Conchita was twitching and whimpering by this time, looking barely human. Lipardo straddled her, then shoved the ice pick hard into the base of her skull, swiftly cutting the spinal cord. The woman stopped twitching before Vennera could stand up.

He picked up the beer bottles, the only items in the apartment that carried his fingerprints, and put them in his pockets.

11

"Salvador, are you awake?"

The voice in Salvador Lirio's ear was that of his wife of sixty years. He didn't even think of pretending to be asleep.

"Yes, Elena?"

"I fear for Angelita."

"Angelita can take care of herself. Even though she has said this since she was fifteen, it may be true."

"She doesn't have her helicopter and her pistol here with her. Don Hector has no helicopters, but he has many men with guns."

"So? Would he dare to do anything to Angelita when he knows how much we think of her? He knows what hold he has over us. Harming Angelita would break it."

In the beginning Gurrola had promised Lirio aid in his old feud with Don Luis Martinez. The aid had given the Lirios victory, so that for a while Don Salvador turned a blind eye to much that the family's "visiting relative" did.

Then things began to happen, like Carmen the maid disappearing. But if Don Salvador complained, as in honor he ought to, Gurrola could say enough to the police to bring disaster to the whole Lirio family.

It was shame and dishonor that was to be feared, above all. The Lirios had been champions of the Hispanics of Chicago for years. They had been accepted by the neighbors in this wealthy Anglo North Shore suburb. They had become far richer and more successful than Don Luis Martinez. They had founded the Instituto de Fraternidad.

They would lose all this, and in their loss, all the Hispanics of Chicago would lose.

Salvador Lirio had known this for years. It was his shame that he hadn't known it when Gurrola came to him. He shouldn't have been bought so easily by the offer to help in winning a battle that he could have won by himself, almost as easily and far more honorably.

In the darkness he groaned.

"Salvador, do you need your medicine?"

"There's no medicine for this pain."

The silence told Salvador that Elena knew what he was talking about.

"So. If Angelita is in danger—"

"Do not say *if*. I know how men look at a woman they want to rape."

Lirio said nothing. There were events in his wife's life that had given her knowledge no woman should know. Therefore she never talked about them. But he had learned over the past sixty years to trust the judgments she made based on those experiences.

"It would be hard to do without scandal or the police. Then Gurrola would lose as much as we would. More, perhaps."

"Gurrola has money and time to go away and start again. We don't. Even if we avenged her honor, would that heal Angelita? Or bring her back to life, if it came to that?''

Lirio could say no more. Visions of horror filled his mind and choked his voice.

His wife let him wrestle with the nightmares for a moment, then put a hand on his shoulder and let it rest there.

Her touch and the silence soothed him. It always had, from the night after their first quarrel so many years ago. It was her way of telling him that she knew that he would do the right thing.

His wife, Lirio reflected, was probably wiser than he. But she had always managed things so that no one besides them knew it, and he wasn't shamed by others knowing that his wife led. Taking Hector Gurrola's friendship was one of the few times he hadn't followed her advice, and now they were in this mess.

''I suppose he wouldn't let her be killed or raped in cold blood,'' Lirio said finally. ''But he might threaten her to make us behave. Could he carry out the threat if she wasn't in the house?''

''Men like Gurrola have a long reach. To be sure, the Army would be angry if an officer vanished. But it takes more than the anger of soldiers bound by law to avenge the victims of people like Hector Gurrola.''

''Then who do we ask for help?''

''We ask no one until Angelita leaves,'' she said firmly. ''Then at least Gurrola's men must get on an airplane and go to where Angelita is, which may be Japan for all I know! She cannot just wind up 'accidentally drowned' in the swimming pool.''

''And then?''

"I think Fredo Guzman's friend, the one you almost didn't tell me about, should be told."

It wasn't horror that choked Lirio this time. It was an insane desire to laugh. Mostly at himself, for believing that he could keep any secrets from Elena.

But why should he believe that trusting Fredo's friend wasn't leaping from the frying pan into the fire? Besides the fact that Fredo seemed to trust him, which wasn't enough in itself, considering some of Fredo's friends....

No, the truth was that he was already in the fire. This man might at least be the frying pan.

ANGELITA LIRIO FINISHED brushing her hair, went into the bathroom and started on her teeth. When she'd rinsed her mouth, she stripped off her bathrobe and underwear and pulled on her pajamas.

They were a depressingly practical pair; gray, opaque, high cut and loose. She'd planned to enjoy wearing something silly, even sexy, to bed on this visit to her grandparents' home.

That idea went out the window at once. It just didn't seem right when she was a guest in their home. It was also a waste, since there was no man around to see her.

Or rather, when there were no men around she *wanted* to see her. That was why she wore her one-piece bathing suit instead of the bikini in the pool, because of Hector Gurrola and his "friends."

Oh, maybe they were real friends, and certainly some of them were handsome enough. All except that little guy, Vennera. He gave her the galloping creeps.

As for the rest—there was just too much mystery about them. Nobody else in the family, even back in Mexico, had ever heard of Gurrola before he showed up.

He and his friends might not be doing anything worse than freeloading, and maybe her grandparents could afford it. But she wasn't ready to bet the price of a drink at the officers' club on it.

It wasn't just the freeloaders, either. It was the way everybody clammed up when she asked about Carmen. Maybe it was just that Carmen had got pregnant and run off, and they were trying to save her reputation. But Angelita had thought she'd at least get a straight answer from her grandfather. She didn't.

And who was that vice cop her father knew? Fredo Guzman—that was the name. She probably wouldn't be able to get a direct line to him, but she could always call up Carlos Luna. Or even better, his wife, Maria.

Angelita turned off the light and crawled under the covers. She didn't think she could do any harm by asking a few questions. If Gurrola had had some good reason for keeping clear of the Lirios until just a few years ago, Fredo would be sure to know.

Charging ahead was always a bad bet. It would be like flying her chopper into a mountain valley in a fog without knowing where the other end was or even if there *was* another end.

Angelita Lirio hadn't made captain at twenty-seven by being that dumb, and she didn't intend to start now.

VENNERA REWOUND THE FILM, pulled the hood over his head and watched the little screen light up.

The hidden camera looked out through a fish-eye lens set in the tile wall of Angelita's bathroom. The tile design was a dazzling mix of reds, oranges and purples. In the middle of that design, a single lens the size of a thumbnail would be hard to find even for someone looking for it.

Angelita had been totally unsuspecting of hidden eyes. She ambled into the bathroom as if she had nothing whatever on her mind except a good night's sleep. She picked up her toothbrush, squeezed out the paste, brushed her teeth, and then— Ah, then!

He stopped the picture as Angelita's panties dropped to the floor, to savor her. Maybe there were better angles, and maybe he would find out, but right now he would say she looked very fine as she was.

He started the picture again to savor other things, such as the sway of her breasts and the positively glowing thighs....

A pity that she wasn't to be touched—for now. But patience was worth it when the prize was a woman like this. Angelita's time would come. After all, she had inquired about Gurrola, hadn't she? The next thing she would do would be to tell someone who shouldn't know it that Hector Gurrola might not really be a relative of the Lirios.

After that, it would be only a matter of time.

GROGAN'S BAR AND GRILL was in an Irish neighborhood called Bridgeport. Grogan sat across from Mack Bolan at a table in one of the back rooms.

The warrior raised his glass of Bushmills. "To Ireland, free and united ever more!"

The owner repeated the toast and chugged so much of his own whiskey that it didn't register that Bolan only sipped his.

"It's not surprised I am, for the word was out to the boys a few days ago. The Justice men are lookin' for a man come across the water to find new friends for our folk. But what is it you're wantin'?"

"Precious little from you, and that at a good price," Bolan replied. He couldn't pretend to genuine Irish speech patterns, so Brognola was circulating the rumor that he was an Irish-American who'd returned to the old country and taken up the fight for freedom there.

"You understand we'll not be letting you have even that without sendin' word to Boston to be sure you're who you say you are. It would not be the first time the Justice men have tried to put one across us. Maybe if they find what's left of the ones they send often enough, they'll stop."

"Maybe, but I won't be one of them. Would you believe the boys who sent me know as much about the Justice as you do? And would you believe that it's because of that I'll be on my way as soon as you give me some names."

"Names?"

"Names, and not a one of them in the IRA or even, likely enough, Irish."

Grogan took a hefty gulp of the Bushmills. "What's the world coming to? Aren't Irishmen good enough to fight for the freedom of their own land anymore?"

"It's not a matter of good enough. There's plenty of people ready to help Ireland's fight. The names of a few of them have reached our ears even across the water." Bolan named several crime lords who had a reputation for terrorist connections. Grogan nodded encouragingly.

"I'm here to be visiting them, one by one. In Chicago it's one Hector Gurrola. Now, if you know as much of the man as you seem to, would you care to arrange a meeting with him for me?"

Grogan frowned. Bolan decided to let the man refuse before offering a bribe. Seeming too eager could make even someone as unimaginative as Grogan suspicious.

"I can do that when we know who you are."

"By all the saints, man! Do you think the Justice Department makes the fuss they've made over innocent men?"

"No. But they've made it over men who turned out to be working both sides of the fence. I'm not saying you're on tomorrow's list for a kneecapping until we've called Boston, but—"

"Are you afraid of Gurrola?"

"Afraid of a bloody greaser with his hands dripping cocaine? Are you after insulting a man whose whiskey you've drunk?"

Grogan had drunk about four times as much Bushmills as Bolan, and seemed to be ready for a fight. Bolan remembered the size of Grogan's two bouncers and decided to avoid a confrontation if he could. The local IRA network might be on his tail if he took out Grogan and the bouncers.

"I'll drink more of it to show that I'm not aiming to insult you," Bolan said, refilling his glass. It didn't take much, and he was able to go on sipping as they drank several more toasts to various Irish persons and causes that Bolan had never heard of. By the time the glasses were half-empty, Grogan seemed in a better mood.

"Now, I'm not saying that I can be bought. But if you're really after nothing but an introduction to Gurrola—"

Bolan swore an impressive collection of oaths that he'd picked up on his missions in Ireland. At least it impressed Grogan.

The bar owner nodded. "Then I can see my way to giving it if you make it worth our while. You see, we're past due on our next shipment to the old country. Some of our suppliers came up short."

Bolan kept a straight face. He *was* going to be called in to help with the shortage that he'd created that night in Decatur.

"Guns or explosives?"

"Man, did I say what the shipment was?"

"No, but I don't think the lads in Belfast asked you for Barbie dolls and GI Joe figures!"

"GI Joe figures!" Grogan roared with laughter. Bolan began to think that taking out the man and his bouncers might be a good idea, after all, just on general principle. Behind the facade of a hard-drinking, jolly Irishman, he was feeding the brutal war in Northern Ireland.

But Grogan and his bouncers were small fish compared to Gurrola, Lipardo and their dreams of a Chicago cocaine empire. Catching small fish and letting sharks get away was no way to run a war.

Getting the joke out of his system sobered Grogan. "We need explosives more than guns. The—well, the way we have of getting guns is fairly reliable. But the other stuff..."

"Five hundred kilos of plastique and fifty fuses?"

"Tempting. What kind of fuses?"

"Any mix you want, although we're a bit short of radio-command ones."

Grogan was sweating by the time they finished the details of delivery and security. The back room was thoroughly air-conditioned; it was greed and whiskey, not heat, that made him sweat.

Bolan hoped that Grogan had plenty of Bushmills on hand when the IRA found out what he'd sold them as plastic explosive and fuses. The explosive would stand anything short of a chemical analysis, but no fuse in the world would make it do more than give off a cloud of stinking smoke. The fuses would mostly go "pop" or "fizz" rather than "bang," except for a few that would go off like grenades when somebody tried to set them.

A few IRA explosives experts were going to be missing fingers or faces after the shipment reached Ulster. If the word spread, there'd be men coming after Mr. Grogan to see that he was missing a lot more.

That was a pleasant thought. So pleasant, in fact, that Bolan smiled at the bouncers as he made his way out through the barroom with the introduction to Hector Gurrola in his pocket.

12

The Executioner looked in the rearview mirror to make sure his tail was still there. The black Firebird had dropped back about fifty feet since they'd left the Northwest Tollway, but its driver hadn't given up.

Bolan had taken the Tollway well out toward Rockford before cutting back toward the North Shore suburb where the Lirios lived. Somewhere just beyond the city limits, the Firebird slipped into his rearview mirror. Before they'd covered another five miles, Bolan knew he was being tailed.

Who was it? Both the police department and the criminals in the area probably had some sort of a description of him. So the tail might be on the side of the law.

Whoever the tail belonged to, Bolan had to get rid of it. His chances of dealing with Gurrola would be ruined if he showed up with someone tagging along behind.

Bolan's rented car couldn't outrun the black sportster. Even if it could, the guy could phone in for backup. And Bolan wouldn't find out who had ordered the tail.

He slowed his vehicle, letting the Firebird close in, trying to get a good look at the driver. The man looked medium sized, wearing a sports jacket and a thoroughly unmemorable face.

No clues there. Bolan accelerated slightly and started looking for pull-offs or all-night service stations.

The only thing that showed up was an unpaved side road. He turned onto the road and waited until the Firebird also made the turn, then waited another minute until the headlights showed a long straight stretch of road ahead. Not only long and straight, but with no deep ditches on either side.

Bolan cut off the lights, slowed the car to a crawl, popped the driver's door and rolled out onto the shoulder of the road. The car rattled on another hundred feet until a wheel hit a dip and bounced it into a left turn. It rolled off the road and bumped into a massive hedge.

The warrior wore a dark turtleneck and black slacks; it was even odds on the tail's having seen him bail out. He kept low as the Firebird rolled up, the Desert Eagle in his hand.

The Firebird passed him, slowing as the driver spotted Bolan's stopped car. As the Firebird also stopped, Bolan drew down and sent a .44 slug into both rear tires.

Under the twin hammerblows, the car jumped like a stung horse. The driver vanished. Bolan heard a thump on the far side of the car; he must have gone out the passenger side.

The warrior vaulted the hedge and began working his way toward his car. The man would be headed that way, which made it the best place for an ambush. It would also be a good idea to protect his own car. The

Firebird wasn't going anywhere again tonight, and missing the meeting with Gurrola was a bad idea.

In the darkness of a cloudy country night, even Bolan's superb night vision couldn't show him a gap in the hedge until he was almost on top of it. He was also a good thirty feet beyond the car.

He crawled through the gap, sank up to his elbows in smelly muck, but managed to avoid making enough noise to alert the tail. The man was now examining the driver's side of the car with a pencil flashlight in one hand and what looked like a .45 in the other.

Bolan reached the passenger side of the car while the man was on the driver's side. Then in one smooth sequence of movement, Bolan rose to a crouch, jerked the door open and aimed the .44.

"Freeze!"

The man had the sense to obey.

"Drop your gun."

The .45 thumped to the seat.

"Assume the position!"

The man spread-eagled himself against the car as Bolan walked around it, the big muzzle of the Desert Eagle threatening the man every step of the way.

Bolan patted him down, looking particularly for badges, then pulled his wallet and checked it out. A few bills, two credit cards, a photograph of a plump but pretty blonde, but nothing suspicious, nothing to prove this man deserved to die.

"Take off your tie and belt." The man complied, the business end of the Desert Eagle still a convincing argument.

"Now your jacket." The man shrugged himself out of the jacket and held it out to Bolan with one hand.

As he did, the other hand disappeared into the tail of the jacket.

Bolan's reflexes threw him into movement. He hurled the tie and belt into the man's face, leaped to the left and fired low.

The heavy slug ripped into the man's leg just above the knee, spinning him around. It went on to punch into Bolan's car, rocking it on its wheels.

The man was game enough to try to bring up the .25 automatic he'd slipped out of the jacket. Bolan didn't waste another round; he closed in on the man and twisted the little weapon out of his hand, then punched him in the jaw.

The lights and shooting hadn't attracted any attention so far, but that wouldn't last. Bolan hauled the man back to the Firebird and dumped him in the back seat, with the wounded leg high to reduce pressure. Then he backed his own car around, out of the hedge and back onto the road.

He'd call from the first public telephone he found, giving the Firebird's location. Then on to Gurrola's house, where he wouldn't even be very late, and he'd have a good story to tell.

It was just remotely possible that he'd put somebody from the law in the hospital tonight. But the man wasn't in the grave, and he'd behaved like someone who didn't care about mistaken identity. Fortunately for him, he'd met the Executioner, who did.

The incident would make a good story for Gurrola's ears. Turn him into an IRA man trying to trail Bolan to the explosives and set up a hijacking. Then point out that if Grogan's people were like that, the Provos would be happy to deal with almost anybody more honest. Gurrola could even pass the story on when he went to Europe.

It was odds against his ever getting that far. If he did, though, it would be more trouble for Mr. Grogan.

BOLAN STOPPED BESIDE the Lirios' main garage and killed the engine. Then he climbed out of the car and waited empty-handed as Jimmy Vennera approached.

Pure gut instinct told him to draw the .44 and erase the man on the spot. Conchita's death was only the latest stop on the man's trail of horror. At least five other women were dead because of him, and a dozen more lived with nightmares.

Bolan's hands didn't even twitch. But in his mind a resolution turned to steel. Conchita would be the last stop on the Bedbug's bloody trail.

"Good evening," Vennera said. "You're late."

"I almost didn't make it at all." Bolan was curt, the manner of a man accustomed to speaking to the top dog and not wasting time with underlings.

"Has—"

"If Don Hector wants you to help find the people who delayed me, I'm sure he'll tell you. In fact, I'll ask him to let you help. I've heard of you."

Vennera took that as a compliment. He led the way toward the entrance to the swimming-pool pavilion. Over the crunch of gravel, Bolan heard a window squeal as it rose.

He looked toward the sound. A woman was standing in the window, wearing pajamas. She seemed to feel the eyes on her and drew back.

Vennera laughed unpleasantly. "That is Angelita, La Principesa. She's much woman, but not for you or me. They say," he added.

"I don't play where I work," Bolan told him. "I don't like watching my back when I have my pants off."

"Very wise," Vennera agreed. His voice shrank to a whisper. "But if I offered to watch your back, and you mine, so that we might take turns with La Principesa . . . ?"

Bolan gave a jerky nod. He didn't trust his voice. The hardman took this as agreement and laughed again.

ANGELITA SAT ON THE BED in her darkened bedroom, legs drawn up almost to her chest. She wondered where her brain was, letting the Bedbug get a look at her.

The dirty feeling of having his eyes on her faded. In its place was a memory of the man with him—big, powerful, moving with a certain grace.

Another of Gurrola's friends? Maybe. But he might be something else. She'd seen him looking at the Bedbug when the little man was obviously describing her charms. His face was a frozen mask of disgust, or maybe rage.

He didn't like Vennera. Did that mean he was a friend of Mad Fredo's? Not that all Fredo's friends were people a woman could rely on—but just maybe this man could be a solution instead of another problem.

HECTOR GURROLA HAD A suite of his own—bedroom, guest room, study and bath—carved out of what had been the children's wing. Bolan noted that it was far enough from the owners' suite, the guest rooms and the servants' quarters for peculiar comings and goings to pass unnoticed.

Bolan took a chair that gave him a good view of the door and a clear line of escape to the window. He didn't want to turn his back on either Gurrola or Lipardo, who sat on an antique dining-room chair by the door.

Was it recognition or just suspicion that he saw in the top soldier's eyes? The million-dollar bounty on Bolan's head was common knowledge among criminals all over the world. At least his cover identity made it plausible that he wouldn't sit with his back to a door or an armed man.

They began with small talk. Gurrola obviously believed in aping upper-class Spanish manners, and not being too quick to talk of business.

After half an hour, the drug lord suddenly broke off his praises of the Lirios' hospitality and said, "But I'm sure this begins to bore you, though you are too polite to say so. What brings you to me?"

Bolan began his story. A faction of the IRA no longer trusted outside weapons suppliers. They wanted to find a way of raising money for weapons themselves. What better way than drugs?

"Indeed, what better way?" Gurrola repeated. "If it's good enough for the CIA, why should it not be good enough for us?" He smiled.

"I wouldn't argue with that," Bolan said, pretending pleasure at this meeting of minds. "The question is our getting the drugs. The European drug kings seem to want to stay out of politics. Even the biggest of them isn't much, anyway."

"You've approached the Colombians, I trust."

"Not in any way that you'd have heard of, but yes, we have," Bolan said. He shrugged. "It's not politics that holds them back. They don't think we'd know the business."

"You disagree?"

"I've got the names of twenty likely lads. Understand, you won't get them for a while. But I wouldn't be here if I didn't have them all champing at the bit."

"I won't say you're the answer to my prayers, because truthfully I'm a very poor churchgoer," Gurrola stated. "But you certainly may be an answer to the overstock of cocaine we'll have before the year is out. Even when one expects to be the supplier for every crack shack in a great city, there are only so many crack shacks."

Bolan saw Lipardo raise eyebrows at his chief's exaggeration. Lipardo, he suspected, was a bit more cautious than his boss about telling lies that could be traced.

But Gurrola seemed to think that Bolan was greedy enough to follow any lead that held out hope of financial independence for him and his faction of the IRA.

"I think we can do business," Gurrola said, signaling to Lipardo. The man produced a bottle of brandy and three glasses.

"I think we can even drink to our mutual success. But I need some evidence of your good faith. Some evidence that needs no transatlantic phone calls or similar activities that the police can trace."

Gurrola went on, explaining about a traitor in his own organization who'd vanished in the face of an attempted hit. Bolan quickly recognized Enrique Dino.

"If you can bring me this man, you'll find me ready to provide the cocaine for your people," Gurrola concluded.

"You expect a stranger in town to do better than your men have done."

"Are you saying my men don't know their business?"

"I'm sure they do. In this matter, better than I would."

Gurrola laughed. "Ah, I was right in setting you this test. You know that information is nine-tenths of a successful hit.

"I'm not asking you to go blind. All that I know about this man and those who might be his friends, you will know also. Only then will I expect you to go to work."

"How soon will this be?"

Bolan went on to remind Gurrola about the rumors of Justice Department interest in him. This gave him an excuse for appearing eager.

"Two days," Gurrola replied. "Be back here then, about ten o'clock at night."

ANGELITA HAD ON A BATHROBE now, so she didn't hesitate about going to the window when she heard the footsteps crunching on the gravel. She watched Vennera walk with the big man to his car.

They stood and talked for a couple of minutes, too quietly for her to overhear. But she could see the big man's face more clearly. She used the time to memorize his features.

She also saw a look of distaste on his face as he listened to Vennera, as if he were smelling an open sewer. It only faded when he cut the man off in what looked like midsentence and climbed into his car.

Vennera was still standing in the parking lot when the car's taillights disappeared down the driveway.

Angelita crawled back into bed. This time she wasn't shivering. She was past that. She was too busy solving a tactical problem.

The stranger looked as suspicious as any of Gurrola's friends. But it was still worth asking Fredo Guzman about him. In fact, he might be more willing to talk about the man than about Carmen. If he was willing to talk at all. And if he wasn't, did she have a way to make him?

No. Her self-respect aside, Fredo wasn't open to that kind of bribe. He might be mad, he might sometimes be a little careless about who got in the line of fire, but he wasn't the Bedbug.

He wasn't too picky about who helped him, either. Her grandfather might fuss that it wasn't a woman's job to put herself in danger. Fredo didn't care who put themselves where if it helped him put a few more criminals in jail or the morgue.

In this, at least, Mad Fredo might be wiser than her grandfather.

BOLAN'S TELEPHONE RANG.

"Hal. You got what I asked you for on Captain Lirio?"

"I called in a few favors at the Puzzle Palace to get her file pulled. Would you believe she's the kind of straight arrow I thought they didn't make anymore?" Brognola went on to recite an impressive military career that included commendations for leadership, awards for flying and efficiency reports that made Angelita sound like somebody who could walk on water.

Bolan knew that efficiency reports and awards were inflated these days. Still, a captain with that kind of record had to be something special. She didn't seem to care about anything except flying, so even if she'd been a man she wasn't the kind of officer who made general. But it seemed as impossible as anything could be that she'd have anything to do with Hector Gurrola.

"Glad to hear that," Bolan said. "The old couple is going to have a rough enough time as it is, without their Principesa being involved in Gurrola's business."

Brognola said goodbye a minute later, leaving Bolan looking in his imagination toward a luxurious mansion on the North Shore. Toward where Angelita Lirio had probably finished her morning run and was sitting down to breakfast, innocent of what was happening around her.

Innocent. That was the most important thing about her now. She might be a first-class helicopter pilot, but in this kind of war she was an innocent. She had to be protected while she was in her grandparents' house, and the sooner she left it, the better.

Bolan wondered if he could arrange to have her leave canceled. But Brognola might not be able to push the U.S. Army's bureaucracy fast enough.

Her sudden departure might also make her grand-parents suspicious, and that could drag them into the line of fire. Could he contact her in his cover identity as a foreign terrorist and warn her off? Maybe, but that might just make her more suspicious, more stub-born and more ready to run into danger. The United States Army didn't teach its officers to run away from fights.

Drawing the fight away from innocent bystanders was one thing. Drawing the fight away from some-body trying hard to get into it was something else, like a first-class headache for Mack Bolan.

13

It was the third day since Bolan received the information that was supposed to lead him to Enrique Dino. The information turned out to be quite a haul. Hal Brognola warned Bolan that he was now having trouble keeping his friends in the Justice Department from jumping the gun.

Bolan wished him success. Gurrola might be too eager to hit the big time, and that was about to be fatal. But as long as he was alive, he was intelligent enough to be dangerous. If he had any sort of advanced warning, he could be dangerous to more people than Bolan.

Meanwhile, the Executioner had his own troubles. He was running out of excuses for not producing Dino, alive or dead. He was also running out of patience with Fredo Guzman, who couldn't seem to give him a date for the big yachting party.

Bolan wanted to hit that party, and hard. It would be the best way of cleaning out the Lirios' "long-lost relative" and his friends without danger to the family or servants.

But either Langas wasn't going or Guzman wasn't talking. Bolan was toying with the idea of simply taking out Langas and what was left of his gang. That would force Guzman onto another assignment, and let Bolan get on with his.

But Guzman was still a professional, trained observer, close to the scene of the action and able to take care of himself. That made him too valuable to be casually thrown away.

The telephone rang.

"Hello."

"I think I need to talk to you," Angelita Lirio said.

"I suspect that we do need to talk," Bolan said. "Where are you calling from?"

"Outside the house."

"Far enough outside the house that you're not likely to be tailed?"

"Not likely."

"All right. I'll meet you at the White Hen at the corner of Route 98 and Thornton Road at eleven-thirty."

BOLAN PARKED HIS CAR a hundred yards from the White Hen and approached the store by a meandering, zigzag route. He cut across fields and through hedges, and generally tried to look like part of the landscape whenever he wasn't moving.

Halfway to the store he recognized Angelita sitting at the wheel of her Mercedes. He also saw a car parked on the shoulder of the exit from Route 98 with two men occupying the front seat.

Bolan studied them through his nightscope. They looked like two hardmen, probably the mobile force to block Angelita's escape. If they'd wanted to kill her, she would probably already be dead. So it was either a snatch or maybe just observing who she met.

If it was observing, maybe only two men were required. But if it was a snatch... Bolan tried to put himself in the place of the men's boss. Where would he put at least two more men for a nice quiet approach to the Mercedes? Assuming that he couldn't be sure in advance where the car would park, or whether Angelita would resist?

One behind the store, he decided. Probably in a patch of well-grown bushes that would hide him from the casual eye. And one on the roof with a long-range weapon to cover Angelita or anybody they needed to keep from interfering.

Bolan crawled toward the bushes. Attacking from the rear would take him out of sight of Angelita for a bit, so he'd have to work fast. Also quietly, so that the man on the roof wouldn't learn that his friend was dead until it was too late.

Fifty feet from the bush, Bolan knew that he'd guessed right. Someone in dark clothes crouched just outside the light from the store's rear door. A shapeless form that ended in a pair of jogging shoes crouched on the roof.

Bolan threaded the silencer onto the Beretta, then drew his Gerber combat knife and continued on. Now the warrior was near enough to hear the hardman's breathing.

At twenty-five feet the hardman seemed to sense something. He rolled over, looking to the left. Bolan shifted right, crouched and leaped.

He came out of the darkness like a Panther, knife in hand. The man twisted, raising a snub-nosed revolver. Bolan slammed down on top of him, left hand gripping the gun wrist, right hand driving the knife up under the man's chin. The point reached his brain; he spasmed and died.

The almost-silent killing still drew the man on the roof. As he peered over the edge, Bolan rolled, pulling the dead hardman on top of him. Confronted by his friend apparently grappling with Bolan, the man on the roof hesitated.

Bolan didn't. The 93-R coughed discreetly, and the second man's head snapped back, his AR-15 clattering onto the gravel.

The next sound the warrior heard had him up and running. A car, probably the mobile reserve's, was approaching the store. He sprinted around the end of the building, fitting the shoulder stock as he moved.

He could have saved time going through the store. But the people coming up wouldn't hesitate to shoot into the store to get Bolan. He couldn't move the whole fight away from the White Hen, but he could control where the bullets went.

The car pulled up beside the Mercedes. One of the hardmen was now in the back seat, aiming his autorifle at Angelita.

But when the woman spotted Bolan, she threw open the door and dived out of the vehicle, hitting the ground hard, rolling but staying down. The gunner sprayed the Mercedes with 5.56 mm slugs, and the windows disintegrated. So did the rifleman's head, as Bolan fired a round from the .44 that was dead-on.

The driver had less courage or more discretion. He burned rubber backing up, then swerved, going up on two wheels. He was accelerating toward the Route 98 entrance when the Desert Eagle boomed again.

A tire blew, sending the car skidding sideways. It made a half turn and rammed backward into a sign. The gas tank erupted, and a fireball enveloped both the car and its driver.

"Come on!" the warrior shouted.

"Where are we going?"

"We'll decide that when we're out of here. The fewer people who can recognize us, the better."

They stopped for a moment behind the store, so Bolan could shoot out the rear light. Somebody who'd just opened the back door had second thoughts; Bolan heard the door slam.

He shone his flashlight on the two dead hardmen. "Recognize either of them?"

"The one behind the bush. I've seen him with Gurrola's right-hand man a few times. And I recognized the two men in the car."

"All from the house?"

She nodded. Then she gripped Bolan's arm so hard that her nails dug into his skin through the blacksuit, closed her eyes and threw up.

"Sorry," she said, wiping her mouth with the back of her hand.

Bolan nodded. Reactions to one's first firefight took every possible form and a few most people would believe impossible until they actually got shot at. Angelita wasn't the first officer he'd seen throw up the first time they'd had bullets aimed at them.

They'd also been as embarrassed as Angelita was, until they realized that nobody thought the worse of them. Bolan knew all she needed now was a little time to pull herself together.

They'd been in the car for twenty minutes, heading for Rockford, when Angelita spoke.

"Thanks isn't really adequate. If I think of something that is, I'll say it. But—thanks." She pulled a package of wash-and-dries out of her shoulder bag and began to wipe her face.

When she'd finished, she looked at the road signs. "Where are we going?"

"That depends."

"On what?"

"On a number of things."

"What are they? Mr.—"

"Bruning. Milo Bruning."

"That's what I thought. Mr. Bruning, the Congress of the United States trusted me with a commission in the United States Army. My superior officers trust me with some very expensive helicopters. How about you trusting me to answer your questions intelligently?"

"I will, when I'm sure I can ask them intelligently. Let's start with the obvious one. Did you tell anyone where you were going?"

"No. Just that I was going for a drive."

"Then either you were tailed or my phone's been tapped."

She grimaced.

"The men we're dealing with are vicious but not stupid," Bolan pointed out.

They drove on in silence for a few minutes. Then Angelita went on. "From what Fredo Guzman said— What's wrong, Mr. Bruning?"

Bolan realized that he'd nearly put them in a ditch. "Maybe nothing. Maybe quite a lot. What did Sergeant Guzman have to say for himself?"

"Not much for himself. Quite a lot about you. That's why I called up and asked for the meeting."

"He convinced you I could be trusted?"

"Yes. He also thought I might work with you. Keep my eyes and ears open, and pass on anything I saw or heard. He convinced me that you wanted to do something about Gurrola, but that you also wanted to save my grandparents' reputation. That's important to me."

"Thanks," Bolan said. He pushed the car up to the legal speed limit.

"What's the hurry?"

"I want to get you to a safehouse I've set up."

"A safehouse? You're CIA?"

"The Company's agents aren't the only ones who need safehouses."

"No, the KGB uses them, too. But somehow I don't think you're working for the Russians." She laughed.

"I'm not working with any one agency," Bolan told her. "I'm working for... Let's call it a special task force that can draw on the resources of a number of different agencies and departments. Anyway, I'm taking you to a safehouse, where you'll be out of danger until I—we've finished with Hector Gurrola."

"I'm in danger?"

"You probably were already, if somebody thought it was worth tailing you then trying to take you out. After tonight it'll be worse. Gang bosses don't lose four of their hit men without trying to find out why.

If the trail leads anywhere near you, you'll have to be out of their reach.''

"That's going to mean dumping my whole civilian wardrobe," she said.

"I think I can arrange to have it replaced. In fact, if you have any leave left when this is over, we can go clothes shopping together."

"Including some more gray pajamas, I suppose?"

Bolan grinned. "That's your decision, Captain Lirio."

What wasn't her decision, or his, was bringing the Justice Department in directly. That was now a life-or-death matter. Enrique Dino was too important as a witness. Angelita couldn't just vanish, nor could she be allowed to walk around making a target of herself.

That meant lots of heavy-footed Justice Department people tramping around. Half of them were always men whose street smarts could fit in a thimble with room to spare. They might scare Gurrola off just when he was all set up for the payoff.

But risking Angelita's life went against everything Bolan had fought for since he'd declared war on the predators. He'd start her at the safehouse in Rockford, where Don Salvador's people should be able to protect her for another forty-eight hours.

After that, it might be a race, with both sides feeding reinforcements in as fast as they could. The winner would be the man who best followed Nathan Bedford Forrest's rule of war: "I just get there first with the most men."

"THE BEDBUG THINKS LA Principesa has betrayed us," Hector Gurrola said.

Danny Lipardo controlled himself with an effort. Naturally Jimmy Vennera was trying to justify himself for sending four Gurrola soldiers to their deaths—not to mention sending them after Angelita.

"She has no knowledge that we need fear," Lipardo replied.

"Are you sure of that?" Gurrola asked. He didn't try to keep the sarcasm out of his voice.

Lipardo wanted to scream the same question at his chief. Or had Vennera gone straight to Gurrola and spoken plainly? Was he trying to change sides, become Gurrola's number-two in return for having Angelita thrown to him like meat to a wolf?

"I'm not sure of much in this world and nothing in the next," Lipardo said. "But she doesn't know anything about the meeting on the yacht. Indeed, I doubt that she knows anything that could make her dangerous to us before that meeting. Forty-eight hours isn't much time."

Lipardo grinned. "So with your permission, boss, I think we should move swiftly against Enrique Dino. We *know* that he has betrayed us and could be dangerous."

Gurrola relaxed visibly. As he did, so did Lipardo. The matter of Vennera could wait if they were in agreement about Angelita Lirio.

Lipardo waited for Gurrola to light a cigar, then dropped his bombshell.

"We can take Dino any time you wish. We know where he is."

"That address in Rockford?"

"Everything checks out."

"I'll take back some of what I've thought about Vennera. We do not want to hide Dino aboard the yacht for more than twenty-four hours before we sail north. Time the snatch on him accordingly."

"As you wish. And with your permission, I'll go myself. It was Vennera who sent the four men after Angelita. But that he was able to send them reflects on my honor for not stopping him."

"We need not discuss your honor, Danny," Gurrola replied, drawing on the cigar. "I have great faith in it. More faith than I have in that man who says he's from the IRA and promised to give us Enrique Dino."

"Shall we take him, too?"

"Don't spend time or men looking for him. But if he turns up in your path, bring him to me. Preferably live, as I would like to ask him some questions. Also, I don't want a feud with the Provos if he is truly associated with them."

Lipardo thought that the tall man's chances of being from the Provos were about the same as Hector Gurrola's chances of being elected Pope. He would obey orders and try to bring the man in alive. But he wouldn't lose any men over it.

14

Fredo Guzman made his way to the stern of the Lirio yacht, then began to walk forward, eyes flicking to right and left.

It was a respectable walk. *Sirena* was a hundred and forty feet long, Italian built, with an aluminium hull and three big diesels able to drive her at twenty-five knots. She was too small for a swimming pool or a helipad, but she had just about everything else Guzman had ever heard of in a luxury yacht.

This included a crew of five, all of them, at the moment, supposedly on a paid vacation. Guzman hoped they'd all done what they'd been told, but he wasn't counting on hopes. So he was doing a check for stowaways.

Not that anybody who stowed away to spy on this mob wasn't a damned fool who'd deserve what he got. But Guzman didn't want to hear what Mack Bolan would say if he put any more innocent people in danger. What the man had said about Angelita was enough.

Guzman had passed the bridge and walked out onto the broad forecastle when somebody called down from the port wing of the bridge.

"Hey! Who the hell are you?"

Guzman turned and held out his hands. "I'm with Langas. Just checking to see if anybody sneaked on board lately."

"That's my job, friend. How about I see you turn around and go back down to your cabin?"

"Have a heart," Guzman pleaded. "It must be ninety down below."

"I'll have a heart," the voice replied, "but maybe you won't if you don't go." Guzman was quite sure the man now had a gun on him.

"Okay, okay. Can't blame me for trying to help, can you?"

"No, as long as you don't do it again. See you."

Guzman threw a last look at the forecastle. It would have looked a lot better under a blue sky with lovely women wearing bikinis or even less sprawled on deck chairs. Gangsters and their bodyguards wouldn't improve the scenery nearly as much.

Five gangsters, when Gurrola arrived. He hadn't yet, and neither had any of his soldiers.

Not quite—there were the three who were going to be substitute crew. But none of the top people, particularly Vennera or Lipardo.

Guzman knew that the Executioner had chopped four soldiers out of Gurrola's strength two nights ago. Maybe the drug lord had something in mind that needed the rest, led by Lipardo and Vennera in person.

BOLAN LOOKED AT HIS WATCH as he backed the car out of the parking spot. He could be in Rockford by midnight without hurrying.

Maybe for once he was overreacting. But his instincts hadn't betrayed him yet. Now they were telling him that the Justice Department's men were going to be too late.

Brognola had been all apologies when he'd called to say that the situation had to be put on hold for another twenty-four hours. Bolan hadn't had to say anything. Both men knew that apologies were no substitute for armed teams that would ensure getting Angelita and Enrique Dino to safety, away from Chicago.

Bolan intended to provide another gun in their defense. He wanted to move in on Gurrola and his followers tonight, instead of mounting guard on the safehouse. Wanted to, but couldn't leave Angelita and Dino protected only by the two men Don Salvador had provided.

A faint thump from the trunk made Bolan listen, then pull to the side and stop. Inside the trunk he found that the gray padded nylon case holding the Weatherby had come untied at one end. He retied the case and closed the trunk.

Two minutes later he hit the expressway and started looking for the signs to Rockford.

ANGELITA LIRIO COULDN'T wait to leave the safehouse. Even the worst transient officer's quarters she'd used were better than this basement room.

The mattress was old and lumpy, and the cotton sheets chafed her skin. The icing on the cake was that the apartment building's furnace was still on, and one of the main heating pipes passed right through her room. She would have stripped down to her underwear or even less if the two men guarding the place hadn't looked in on her occasionally.

She compromised by unbuttoning the top two buttons of her blouse and wiping her neck. She wished that Milo Bruning had thought of leaving her something to read, as well as that Beretta 84-BBL under her pillow. She was going to say something about that, the next time they met.

But she realized it was long odds against her ever seeing him again, once the Justice Department people arrived. It would be one more case of ships that pass in the night. She ought to be used to that now, considering how often it happened in the Army.

Angelita opened another button of her blouse and wiped her neck again, then kicked her shoes off and lay down on the bed.

SIX MEN CLIMBED OUT OF the van and quickly divided up the arsenal. Danny Lipardo made sure that only he and one of his trusted men, Chuck Goggin, carried the Mace bombs. Mace was painful, and Vennera was getting a little too fond of seeing people hurt just for the fun of it.

"Check your gas masks, everybody."

One mask wasn't working. "Okay, Paco," Lipardo whispered. "You have to be the outside man."

"Okay."

The six men spread out to cover the alley from side to side. While Paco covered the front, the five remaining men began to shuffle toward the rear of the apartment building. The alley was dimly lit; by the time they reached the door, they could barely see their van.

Lipardo gave a thumbs-up to the driver at the wheel, which the driver returned. Good. The getaway was secure.

He nodded to Vennera, and the little man descended four steps to the level of the basement and knocked.

"Who's there?" came a voice from inside.

"Your friends," Vennera replied.

"Your names?"

Lipardo drew his pistol and a gas bomb. If the codes weren't the right ones . . .

"Firefly and Dandelion."

There was a moment's silence, then the sound of a lock turning. "Okay, friends. You—"

The man broke off when he saw the masked figures standing in the alley. Before he could slam the door, Vennera shot him. Then Lipardo pitched the Mace cannister through the doorway.

Vennera leaped over the guard's prostrate form, gun in hand, vanishing in the rising cloud of Mace.

ANGELITA ROLLED OFF THE bed at the sound of the first shot. Keeping low, she snatched the Beretta from under the pillow and chambered a round.

What sounded like a stampede of elephants came next, then submachine-gun fire chopped the top half of her door into splinters.

The door flew open, and an object flew inside, trailing smoke. No, not smoke. Mace. She felt it tearing at her eyes and nose and starting to clog her throat.

She fired two shots into the smoke and heard a scream. Then she rolled back toward the wall. If she could just push the bed out from the wall a little, to act as a shield . . .

Whoever had come for her wouldn't be ready for a defense. Then they might have to kill her, which was fine. No, not fine. But better than being a prisoner, if the attackers were the people she suspected.

The Mace was still working. She had to narrow her eyes to slits, and even then tears blurred her vision. Every breath felt as if she were inhaling red-hot sand. Her chest was tight, and she felt ready to vomit.

Bullets chopped into the wall, and plaster dust stung her skin and eyes. A figure vaulted through the door, and she squeezed off two rounds. But half-blind, she could barely aim them. Both chipped plaster.

She couldn't make a sound. She could only writhe like a worm on a hook, arching her body, trying desperately to get her breath back. Then her stomach rebelled.

"Hey! That's Angelita Lirio!" somebody shouted. She had the feeling she'd heard the voice before. "Turn her over so she won't choke on her own puke."

Rough hands rolled her over, not caring that they pushed her face down into her own mess. Even rougher hands jerked off her shoes and ripped her blouse from her shoulders.

"The handcuffs, you idiot!" the same voice snapped. "We want her to look normal."

Normal? What was that? Angelita thought she ought to know, but the world was flowing away from her. It finally vanished in the distance. She never felt the cold steel of the handcuffs going on her wrists or the chain on her ankles.

LIPARDO HASTILY SURVEYED the basement apartment. He wasn't particularly happy with what he saw—Chuck dead, along with the two guards. Enrique Dino was wounded so badly that a lot of time was going to go into first aid. Otherwise he wouldn't live long enough to answer some very pertinent questions.

And Angelita Lirio. It was a stroke of pure good luck to find her here. Unfortunately Vennera had been sniffing around the woman, and he'd already had to haul him off her once.

If he had to do it again, the guns were going to come out. He didn't give a puddle of warm beer for Angelita, but he had to have his orders obeyed. Meanwhile, somebody in the upstairs apartments had undoubtedly called the police.

The van rolled up to the basement stairs. The driver stayed at the wheel while Paco opened the side door. A five-gallon can of gasoline came down the stairs, relayed from one man to the next. "Grab the prisoners and get up the stairs!" Lipardo ordered, as he hefted the can.

In thirty seconds he was the only living man in the cellar. He popped the lid off the can, poured a trail of gasoline out of the kitchen, then a second trail back to the basement stairs.

As he climbed the stairs, he turned and flung a lighted match into the gasoline. The blast flung him up the stairs so hard he nearly knocked himself against the van. Hands reached out and pulled him inside.

With only a little bit of luck, the fire should confuse the Rockford police about who had done what to whom. Long enough, anyway, for the alternate evasion plan to work.

He tapped the driver on the shoulder.

"Head for Wilmette and get on the CB. Tell them we'll meet them offshore."

The Lirios had two yachts, the *Sirena*, moored in Grant Park Harbor, and a small cabin cruiser for day trips docked in Wilmette. The cabin cruiser would be crowded, but they wouldn't need to go all the way into town.

THE EXECUTIONER REACHED the safehouse about the time that the Rockford Fire Department stopped pouring water on the smoking rubble.

"Milo Bruning, working for the *Northwest Letter*," the warrior said to the first fireman he saw. Then he pulled out a small tape recorder and thrust the microphone at the man. "Anybody hurt?"

"Looks like somebody torched the basement apartment. Nobody got out of there. Looks like three men."

Three men. Angelita still had a chance.

"Anybody hurt upstairs?"

"Smoke inhalation and scared silly, but nobody—"

"Hey, Rollie, quit banging your gums with reporters and give a hand!" a lieutenant shouted. The fireman shrugged.

"If you want to talk to anybody, better talk to the loo. Only wait until things cool down a bit, okay?"

"Sure," Bolan replied.

He waited just long enough to be sure that nobody would notice his leaving, then walked back to his car.

From the first public telephone he came to, he made a call to Carlos Luna.

FREDO GUZMAN FELT THE vibration as the big diesels started up. He turned to the man beside him.

"What are they going to do with that?" He pointed at the twenty-five foot cabin cruiser bobbing alongside the yacht. "Sink her?"

When she came out to meet *Sirena*, the cruiser had been so low in the water that Guzman wondered if she was already sinking. Then they unloaded Gurrola's soldiers and the two prisoners.

The man beside Guzman frowned.

"You ask a lot of questions."

"This is my first time aboard a yacht like this."

"Make sure it isn't your last."

"No, wait, Snake," Lipardo said from behind Guzman. "Don't just shut him up. Why are you asking?"

"Well, if we sink her or leave her adrift, somebody's going to notice she's missing. I don't suppose we can pick her up—"

"You mean hoist her aboard," Lipardo told him with a condescending smile.

"Yeah, I guess that's what I meant. Anyway, we can't do it, can we?"

"No. But we can tow her north."

"Tow?" Guzman had nearly said "north." The first clue to where they were going—although not a big one. Chicago was nearly at the bottom of Lake Michigan. A ship could go a little way east, or a long way north.

"Yes, tow. Not so difficult in good weather. And nobody will suspect a thing. After all, this yacht draws too much water to get into many of the small harbors. Why shouldn't we tow the cruiser as a tender?"

Lipardo walked away, leaving Guzman suspecting that he'd just learned something important if he could only translate it.

For once, he wished Carlos Luna was here. Luna had worked on Gulf fishing boats during summer vacations since he was fourteen. When he went into the Marines, he drove an amphibious tractor. He knew about boats, ships and the other things that ran on or in water.

But Carlos was just too damned decent for the sleazy side of undercover work. He'd have long since been blown, then blown away. If he had any sense, he'd tell Mack Bolan everything he knew about *Sirena*, then let the Executioner get on with the job.

The last man aboard the cabin cruiser tossed a rope up onto the yacht's deck. Somebody else tied it around a stanchion. The rope slowly went tight as the big yacht started to move.

Half an hour later they were out of sight of the lights of the North Shore suburbs. A big ore freighter passed them, heading south. When she was out of sight, Guzman went below.

He needed to rack out for a bit. Then he'd start thinking about ways of getting to the radio, or at least getting a message out. He and his friends had a code all worked out. Could he get the key words put into a message that wouldn't make anybody suspicious? Maybe.

Would the prisoners last long enough for the message to bring help? Maybe.

If help didn't come, could Guzman do anything by himself to give them a chance? Possibly.

Two "maybes" and a "possibly." About the usual score for undercover work. With Angelita in the picture, it hurt.

SALVADOR LIRIO WASN'T surprised at the picture the courier service delivered just before dawn. He knew about the fate of the safehouse and its occupants. He doubted that Hector Gurrola knew that he knew.

That the picture was no surprise didn't make it less horrifying. It was the photograph of a woman, tortured to death in ways that Salvador Lirio didn't even want to think about.

Along with the picture was a short note, in handwriting Lirio recognized as Hector Gurrola's.

> Don Salvador,
> Angelita is now in the hands of the men who did this. I pray to God that I can prevent her from suffering the same fate. I also ask your cooperation in keeping silent on this matter for a few days. I will let you know when I wish to speak of it.
>
> Most sincerely,
> Hector Gurrola

Salvador Lirio put the photograph in the pocket of his dressing gown and reclined in the window seat of his study. It wasn't in the old man to keep the kind of silence Gurrola wished. He sighed wearily and wondered whether to show the picture and note to Elena. Such things weren't for most women to know.

But then, Elena wasn't most women. She would be afraid for Angelita, but she wouldn't become hysterical.

Indeed, he had much more to fear if he was silent and she later learned of this. The last time he had hidden such a matter from her was twenty years ago. He hadn't forgotten what had transpired.

It would also help if Elena knew everything he did. It wasn't impossible that he had only a few days to live. If so, he and Elena might go together. His enemies wouldn't spare Elena out of compassion.

But they might spare her, thinking that a woman so old could know nothing and do them no harm. That would be a mistake, although a natural one for anyone who hadn't lived with Elena sixty years.

If Gurrola's bandits made that mistake, then Salvador Lirio might see from beyond the grave the final vengeance on those who had dishonored his house.

15

Hector Gurrola closed the cover over the peephole into the cabin where Angelita lay, then beckoned to Danny Lipardo. They climbed the ladder to the main deck, then onto the forecastle. *Sirena* left a creamy wake across the gentle swell as she cruised north at eighteen knots.

Gurrola began pacing up and down, hands behind his back. He was in shirtsleeves, a Browning Hi-Power riding in a shoulder holster.

Suddenly Gurrola stopped, then turned to face his chief soldier.

"I think we can use the Bedbug to bring Angelita to think kindly of me."

Lipardo had grown up in a neighborhood where someone could get killed for calling another person crazy. He also knew that many of Gurrola's wilder ideas only *sounded* crazy.

"I wish you good luck."

"I won't need luck," Gurrola replied. "What does a woman want most on one who has abused her?"

"His balls for breakfast, for one thing."

"And have you laid a finger on her?"

Lipardo began to see his boss's line of reasoning. "No. She hasn't seen my face, either. She might recognize my voice, though."

Gurrola shrugged. "There are drugs to take care of such inconvenient memories."

"Indeed. But what do we want her to remember?" Lipardo almost held his breath.

"What the Bedbug did to her. And afterward what *I* did to him as punishment."

Lipardo let his breath out. He'd guessed right. "So—you will pose as her savior from the monster?"

"Of course. I won't even sweep her into my arms. That will show respect for her pride. Respecting her pride, avenging her honor—or even letting her shoot the Bedbug herself, after I'm finished with him—"

"Shoot Jimmy?"

"You interrupted me," Gurrola reproved mildly. Lipardo bit his lip. His boss's reaction to the next interruption would not be so mild.

"Forgive me, Don Hector, but I was surprised that you have decided to, ah, dispense with the services of our friend."

"It will be worth it if the prize it wins me is Angelita's hand. Then we will be planted firmly in the Lirios, so firmly that when the old ones die, all that is theirs will swiftly be ours."

There were other grandchildren, Lipardo remembered, but none of them anywhere near Chicago. Married to Angelita, Hector Gurrola could well afford to laugh at anything they could do, or bribe them into doing nothing.

It would be necessary to keep this plan absolutely secret from Vennera until Lipardo decided whether to go along with it or not. Otherwise the little man might try to take out both Gurrola and Lipardo, and the odds were that he would succeed with at least one of them.

If Vennera did go, it would also be necessary to replace him as quickly as possible. Lipardo couldn't be in two places at once any more than the next man. Perhaps the Snake? He was efficient, but was he ruthless enough?

OFF TO THE LEFT OF THE Beechcraft, Bolan saw a large island with a cluster of smaller islands beyond it.

"Beaver Island?" he asked Carlos Luna.

The policeman nodded. "No point in looking there. The water inshore's too shallow, and Beaver's got a lot of tourists."

Scratch another possible destination for *Sirena*. Most people would think that finding a large yacht in what was called a lake would be almost easy. But Lake Michigan was really an inland sea. Visibility came and went. They couldn't trust the pilot to keep quiet if they did anything except fly straight to Charlevoix. The Coast Guard couldn't do anything without evidence of wrongdoing that brought *Sirena* into their jurisdiction, and Bolan didn't have that evidence.

Hal Brognola had it, or would have it in a day or so. Then he might be able to put the squeeze on the Coast Guard for a search.

That still left two problems.

The Coast Guard had to play by the rules. It would be hard to make charges stick against Gurrola unless he was caught with evidence, and if he was monitoring the Coast Guard frequencies, there wasn't much chance of that. It didn't take long to dump weighted bodies overboard, scrub decks and hide guns.

The other problem was time. Every hour they didn't find *Sirena* meant one more hour of Gurrola's mercy for Angelita, one more hour for Jimmy Vennera to inflict wounds that no plastic surgeon could ever remove.

THE THREE MEN SAT ON the V-bunk in the bow cabin of the big racing cruiser. From outside came the sounds of Charlevoix Harbor—outboard motors, generators, rigging twanging in the evening breeze. Offshore they heard the heavy-toned whistle of the Beaver Island ferry as she headed out on her eighteen-mile trip with a load of tourists.

Carlos Luna ran a finger along the southern coast of Michigan's northern peninsula, from the Wisconsin border about halfway to the Straits of Mackinac. "They'll be somewhere in that stretch," he stated.

"Why?" Bolan asked.

"They have to be—" Luna began.

"They don't *have* to do anything to make our job easier," Bolan pointed out.

"I would have to agree," said Sergeant Leonardo Abas, an ex-Marine Salvador Lirio had insisted accompany them. "Never assume that your enemy will make things—"

Luna nearly crumpled the chart, holding on to his temper. "If you two supertroopers will listen for a minute—"

"Sorry," Bolan offered. He was tired and on edge, but it was unusual for him to be short with someone who was trying to help.

The real problem was that too much still depended on Fredo Guzman, who might not even be aboard the yacht. They hadn't heard from him since *Sirena* left Chicago, and the warrior couldn't help but wonder if his cover had held up.

"Mr. Bruning, are you listening?" Abas's voice brought his attention back to the chart. Luna was marking the area again.

"It isn't just a wild guess that *Sirena* will be somewhere there. The Lirios's hunting lodge is in the mountains just north of this stretch of coast. *Sirena*'s cruises usually end up there, and Gurrola will want to make this look like an ordinary cruise. Also, the area has a few towns, but much of it's almost wilderness. If you wanted to anchor and do something that nobody else should see or hear—that's the best part of the lake."

"Unless they've gone right over into Lake Huron and hidden on the Canadian side," Bolan pointed out. The map didn't show the other lake, but the warrior knew that the Canadian shore of it was a maze of islands. A small fleet of yachts could hide there, and a large fleet of searchers hunt them for weeks.

Not to mention that the whole area was Canadian waters, and getting the RCMP in the act would take even more time.

Luna stood. "We'll keep a continuous listening watch on this frequency." He handed the other two men slips of paper. "The code allows Fredo to give position and maybe even who's on board if he has time. Who wants the first watch?"

"I'll take it," Bolan offered.

"Okay. The radio's up on the bridge. Leon, have you checked the supplies?"

"The owner kept his promise," the man replied. "Everything we might need, even a first-aid kit and some good booze for the victory party."

Luna narrowed his eyes. "Please don't say that. It's bad luck."

FREDO GUZMAN'S GAZE ROAMED between the dew-slick deck and the dark shore a half mile to starboard. Nobody was on deck; it was too chilly. On the land a few lights twinkled in the distance.

Guzman walked swiftly forward and knocked on the bridge door. He kept his eyes away from the dark water, which had swallowed Enrique Dino's weighted body a couple of hours ago.

"Oh, it's you," Snake said. "What do you want now?"

"To send a message."

"What kind of message?"

"You know who I work for. What kind of message do you think Langas is sending, now that he's agreed to join Don Hector?"

The Snake smiled, as much as his thin, pock-marked face would let him. "So the old pimp's joined up, has he?"

"Don Hector is a man worthy of great respect."

"Yeah, right. Say, you think that big guy really was the Executioner?"

"I think he might have been. We were six pretty good soldiers, but he ate us up like we were amateurs."

"Hope Langas has enough men left," Snake said. "Don Hector likes everybody to pull their own weight."

"Believe me, we will. That's the reason for the message tonight. Langas wants all our people ready to go when we get back. Now, suppose you let me send it, or do you want to send it yourself?"

He handed the sheet with the frequency and the coded message giving the yacht's location to Snake. The hardman frowned.

"Code?"

"Hey, you think my boss can't find the john when he wants to take a leak? Of course it's code." Guzman lowered his voice. "Tell you what. You send the message and don't say anything about it, and it's worth a free trick from our hottest number."

"Two tricks."

"Come on, that's a five-bill broad you're talking about!"

"Two tricks or no go."

Guzman appeared to be thinking if his boss could stand the price. Actually he was thinking of the risks of knocking Snake out and sending the message himself.

He decided they were too great. Anything suspicious happening on board would send *Sirena* off to a new location.

"Two tricks, then."

Guzman was still on edge. He stayed that way until the message had gone out, repeated three times. Even when he went out, he didn't dare look back, although he expected every second to feel a gun stuck into his spine.

JIMMY VENNERA LIGHTED another cigarette, puffed on it a few times, then thrust it against Angelita's left big toe.

She closed her eyes and clenched her teeth, but she didn't cry out.

The hardman cursed softly. The woman seemed determined to prove she was made of iron. He had done things to her that had made some women beg on their knees for him to stop. The most Angelita did was to bite her lip and to close her eyes.

The little man realized that he actually preferred it when she closed her eyes. With other women he enjoyed seeing the pain, the despair, the terror. He saw nothing in Angelita's eyes when they were open except a cold, malignant hatred.

It might be different if Gurrola would just let him use all of his tricks. But the orders were strict; no permanent damage. In any case he didn't have the electrodes and acids that he had used for a couple of women, even if he had been allowed to use them. Lighted cigarettes, hot curling irons, splinters under the fingernails—they were all improvisations, almost beneath his dignity.

He stepped to the bed, gripped Angelita by the hair and jerked. He was glad to see her wince as she rolled over a little too slowly. Then he reached behind him and picked up the leather strap.

As Vennera wielded the strap, excitement rose in him, and a curious thought struck him. Would a woman dominating him feel the same excitement? And if he then turned the tables on her and had her while she was still excited . . . ?

It would be a fascinating experiment. But not one to risk with Angelita. She was too dangerous; it would be impossible to stop any attack she launched without that forbidden permanent damage. Then he would die for a brief pleasure.

That thought chilled him so thoroughly that it was some time before he noticed that Angelita had fainted.

EVEN THROTTLED DOWN, the cruiser's three big engines generated echoes as she slid under the bridge. A flick of the wheel, and the bow started to swing to starboard into the channel to the open lake.

Once they were clear of the Charlevoix breakwater, Luna opened the throttles wider. The cruiser rose on plane, and a white rooster-tail of foam spouted behind her.

"Course?" Luna asked.

Bolan unfolded the chart. It looked the same as it had four hours ago, except for one critical difference. A red circle now marked *Sirena*'s anchorage off the upper peninsula.

"You know the lake better than I do. What's the best route to get us there before dawn?"

"North until we're clear of the Beavers, then northwest. We can run faster in the lee of the islands, and there's less shipping.

"Only don't bet on getting up there before dawn. This baby may be good for fifty knots in a flat calm. If the lake gets up to its usual tricks, we'll be down to half that."

Bolan nodded. He and Abas went below and began sorting out their weapons and gear. The sergeant had a customized Government Model .45 and a Winchester shotgun. Bolan had his full arsenal, as well as waterproof containers for all three weapons. Other bags held an inflatable raft, scuba gear and an assortment of unpleasant surprises for his quarry. The warrior hoped that Angelita Lirio's captors would leave her unharmed. But with Jimmy Vennera on board, Bolan knew that the chances of that were slim at best.

THE RUBBER RAFT SLIPPED over the side of the cruiser with a faint splash. Mack Bolan snubbed the line around a section of railing, then began lowering his gear into the small boat—scuba gear, wet suit, weapons in their waterproof cases, grenades, knife, night scope, flare pistol, binoculars and the silent electric outboard motor and set of paddles for backup.

Finally he loaded an olive-drab cannister that had cost Hal Brognola nobody knew how many favors from the SEAL. In the cannister were forty pounds of plastic explosives and several fuses.

By the time the warrior lowered himself into the raft, it had only a few inches of freeboard. If the wind rose, he'd be in trouble. But luck was on their side, for once. The calm that had let them cross the whole lake at forty-five knots was supposed to hold until tomorrow afternoon, at least.

The warrior locked the motor in its bracket and pressed the starter. The faintest of purrs, and a few bubbles told him that it was running.

"Cast off," he whispered.

Abas hauled in the line. Bolan steered the raft toward shore as Carlos Luna cautiously advanced the throttles. The three engines rumbled softly instead of splitting the night with a roar.

Somebody aboard *Sirena*, four miles east, might be listening for unexpected noises. It was Bolan's plan that they wouldn't hear any until first light. Then they would be facing a two-pronged attack, from landward and seaward. They'd have more than noise to worry about.

16

Danny Lipardo walked across the deck and climbed the ladder to the bridge. Inside the pilothouse, Snake lay asleep on the couch. An AR-15 lay across his chest, and a box of loaded magazines lay on the deck beside the couch.

At the sound of the bridge door's opening, Snake uncoiled like his namesake and sat up. By the time Lipardo could have reached firing position, the Snake had the AR-15 pointed at his chest.

"Very good," he said approvingly. "Anything to report?"

"Nothing unusual. Nothing on the radar, and I rigged the alarm to go off if anybody closed inside a mile. The commercial traffic's all well out in the lake, I guess."

"Okay. Set the alarm for two miles tonight."

"Hey, you don't want me to sleep?"

"We can get somebody else to split the nightwatch. But two miles it is, or I talk to Don Hector."

Snake pretended to salute. "Aye-aye."

Lipardo looked through the forward window and saw that Gurrola had come out on deck. He wore a blue silk dressing gown and high slippers over red pajamas, and looked completely at peace with the world.

The only discordant note was the shoulder holster with the Browning.

"Take care, Snake. I think this might be our last day here."

"Good."

Lipardo climbed down the ladder and was greeted by Gurrola.

"A beautiful morning, isn't it?"

Lipardo looked at the sky. It was still mostly gray, but a tinge of gold in the east hinted of a clear day.

"That's what the weather report says."

"Ah, Danny. Use your eyes to look at the world around you, not your ears to listen to what others say about it. There's too much beauty in the world to ignore. Fine ships, fair days, lovely women."

"Like Angelita?"

Gurrola smiled. "You read my mind. I think today is the day for beginning my courtship of Angelita." He lowered his voice. "Are you ready to do what is necessary?"

"Of course."

"Who did you have in mind to take Vennera's place?"

"The Snake."

"Ah, an excellent choice. And we can replace the Snake with someone from one of the other gangs. Perhaps the older man with Langas. He seems to have a cool head."

"He has shown one so far. We'll need to test him more, of course, but—"

"Details, details. That sort of thing I can leave to you."

AT THE BOTTOM OF THE forecastle ventilator shaft, Fredo Guzman turned away. He didn't run, which would have made too much noise, but he got away from his listening post as fast as he could. If anybody had come by while he was eavesdropping on Lipardo and Gurrola, he would have been a dead man.

Except, maybe, Vennera.

Could he offer the little man what he'd heard in return for an alliance? If Vennera thought Guzman was guarding his back, would he be more likely to do something that got him killed and generally made trouble aboard *Sirena*?

He probably would, but he might very well do it to Angelita.

No. Jimmy Vennera was too dangerous to innocent people, at the best of times. Give him more rope, and he'd hang others before anyone could hang him.

Guzman walked back to his cabin, oddly at ease with himself. He knew that he wouldn't have made this decision before he met the Executioner. Mack Bolan would leave behind him at least one undercover policeman who now thought things out carefully when innocents might be in danger.

TWENTY FEET BELOW THE surface of Lake Michigan, Mack Bolan was at work.

He wore a closed-cycle SEAL scuba outfit so that no bubbles reached the surface to betray his presence to the casual eye. It would be a casual eye, too. He'd watched the yacht through his binoculars for half an hour before hitting the water. Nobody seemed to be keeping any sort of a lookout.

A rubber float bobbed just below the surface, holding most of his arsenal out of sight but ready to hand. He was attaching the explosives and fuses to *Sirena*'s hull, close to her rudder and propellers.

The explosives made two charges, each with its own fuse. One had a time fuse, set for half an hour. The other had a pressure fuse, still on the top-secret list, that had cost Hal Brognola another batch of favors to the Navy.

It reacted to changes in the water pressure. If the men aboard the luxury ship started her engines, the propellers would send water flowing over the fuse. This change in the water pressure would detonate the charge.

Either charge was enough to blow a gaping hole in the hull, besides disabling her rudder and propellers. She might not sink unless both of them went off, but she wouldn't be going anywhere.

That was more important than sinking her, at least to start with. A few innocent people were aboard and had to be snatched free before Bolan could really open up. Otherwise he would have blown *Sirena* out of the water and picked off any survivors as they tried to swim ashore.

Bolan thrust the pressure fuse into the first charge and attached it to the hull. He attached the second charge to the other side of the keel, then checked his watch. He set the fuse for twenty-five minutes instead of half an hour. It had taken him a little longer than he'd expected to set the charges. The time-fuse was supposed to go off when Luna and Abas showed up.

The warrior dived to forty feet, pulling his arsenal with him. His fins beat the gray water as he headed for the little cabin cruiser riding to her anchor a hundred yards from *Sirena*.

LOOKOUT DUTY ON THE CABIN cruiser was the dullest job going. The lookout had done it twice before, and it wasn't getting any better.

He stood up—cautiously because the boat was so small that his hundred sixty pounds could make it rock—then walked to the stern, holding on to the railing every step of the way.

He thought Don Hector was loco to go to all this trouble for a meeting. Water was to drink and wash with, not to travel on. You went traveling on water, and where did you wind up? Miles from nowhere. Miles from good liquor, a hit of marijuana, women...

Ah, well. Nobody ever died of boredom or horniness. They sometimes did die of smart-mouthing Hector Gurrola, particularly if they did it where Lipardo or Vennera heard them.

The bored lookout sat down on the stern seat. As he did, he turned his back to the shore.

A black-clad figure shot out of the water on the shoreward side of the tender, and a long sinewy arm wrapped around the lookout's throat, cutting off his wind. Then the figure plunged back into the water, taking the man with him.

The lookout had just time to stop feeling bored, when the air in his lungs ran out. He inhaled a great gulp of Lake Michigan, a few bubbles trickled out of his mouth and nose, then the black-clad figure dragged him down.

The Executioner watched *Sirena* for a minute to see if anybody on deck had noticed anything. Then he hauled himself swiftly and quietly over the side, pulled his weapons in after him and began unpacking the Weatherby.

LIPARDO WATCHED HIS BOSS go below with a vast sense of relief. His chief seemed to know that time was getting short. Lipardo was on his rounds when he noticed that the lookout in the tender wasn't in sight. That had happened before, but he now remembered that the man hadn't been in sight ten minutes ago, either. He wasn't supposed to stay in the cabin that long.

And was something floating just beyond the tender? Lipardo walked faster than ever back to the pilothouse.

"Snake, the binoculars!"

"Here."

Lipardo focused the glasses and studied the tender. Nothing unusual there, but something that looked like the lookout's baseball cap bobbed on top of the water. He brought the glasses back to the tender. The cabin curtains were drawn, and they hadn't been ten minutes ago.

"Get on the radio to the tender!"

"Eh?"

"The cabin cruiser, you idiot!"

"Okay, okay."

Snake picked up the microphone. "Snake calling the cabin cruiser. Snake calling the cabin cruiser. Come in, cabin cruiser. Wake up, there."

Snake went on trying to raise the lookout for nearly three minutes. By then Lipardo had checked both his guns and was jacking a round into the AR-15.

Finally a voice came back, speaking roughly in Texas-accented Spanish.

"Everything's okay. What's the problem?"

"Nothing," Lipardo replied. "We just didn't see you for a while. We thought you might have gone swimming."

"Me, go swimming in this water? No way."

"Thanks," Lipardo said.

"That doesn't sound like Tico."

"No, it doesn't. I'm going to take the dinghy and check it out. You cover me with the rifle."

"All by ourselves?"

"It might be nothing. Even if there is a problem, do you want the boss to think we can't handle it without crying for help when we don't even know what it is?"

"Put it that way, no."

"Good. I would call for help if I didn't trust you and your rifle."

"Thanks."

Lipardo clapped Snake on the shoulder, then scrambled down to the main deck. The inflatable dinghy bobbed at the foot of the boarding ladder aft. In five minutes he could be out to the tender, see what Tico had been drinking—or find out what else had happened.

Looking forward, he saw the muzzle of the AR-15 poke out of the pilothouse window.

MACK BOLAN SAW THE SAME thing. The man heading aft toward the dinghy might eventually be a threat. The man in the pilothouse was one right now.

He decided to wait, to let the first man get into the dinghy, or at least onto the boarding ladder. Then he'd be an easier target. He looked like Danny Lipardo, and taking him out would be an even better start to the final payoff.

Bolan shifted slightly and reached for the radio. Switching frequencies, he spoke softly into the microphone.

"Cabstand to cabdriver. Time to bring the taxis around. Good weather."

That was the signal to Carlos Luna to get the boat underway at full speed. It also meant that Bolan was in a position to keep *Sirena*'s decks clear with the Weatherby.

He sighted on the barrel of the AR-15, then shifted until the rifleman's face was centered in the cross hairs. One, two, three—take a breath and let it out slowly as the finger contracted on the trigger....

A burst of rifle fire shattered the window and chewed splinters out of the cabin roof. Bits of glass stung Bolan's cheek.

The rifleman was good enough to spot him, but not good enough to keep the AR-15 from riding up. Now he was crouching at the window, trying to see if he'd hit anything.

A pistol cracked three times, which had to be Lipardo. At a hundred yards the average pistol was nothing to worry about, even in the hands of a good shot. Bolan centered the cross hairs again and this time squeezed off a shot.

The face in the pilothouse window vanished as if the man had fallen through a trapdoor. The AR-15 clattered to the deck.

Bolan quickly shifted his sights to get off a shot at Lipardo, but the man was already diving behind a locker.

With no human enemies in sight, the Executioner used two shots to wreck the yacht's radar. Then he punched a hole in the dinghy and watched it bubble down out of sight.

He'd killed the marksman and forced everybody else to stay under cover. Time to reload.

That task completed, Bolan shifted position slightly and crouched, waiting—waiting for someone to try picking up the AR-15, for *Sirena* to get underway, or for his allies to show up.

LIPARDO THOUGHT BRIEFLY of staying where he was to keep the sniper pinned down with the odd pistol shot, then quickly decided otherwise. He needed to be in the pilothouse, where he could warn everybody and coordinate their defense. With two or three soldiers to occupy the sniper, somebody could retrieve the AR-15. A couple more could bring the other rifles and submachine guns aboard into action.

The sniper was good—better than Snake, obviously. But even if he was the Executioner, he wasn't Superman. As well, the cabin cruiser was made of fiberglass and plywood, and it had a gasoline engine. Gasoline burned nicely. The Executioner would burn even more nicely—or go overboard and be slaughtered in the water.

The only flaw he could see in this plan was that there'd be nobody to keep an eye on Vennera. He'd just have to hope that the man wasn't yet suspicious.

Lipardo crawled out from behind the locker and kept below the level of the railing until he reached the door to the main saloon. Then he ducked inside, crossed to starboard and ran forward, shouting.

"Everybody, stay below! We're being sniped! Stay below until I tell you to come up. Then come up on the starboard side. That's the right side, facing forward," he added for the sake of the men who didn't know anything about boats.

He slipped into a crouch as he reached the ladder to the bridge. It's steps were gritty with shattered glass. The bullet that killed Snake had kept on going, out the other side of the pilothouse.

Lipardo reached the pilothouse and spared only a single look at his former subordinate. Part of his face was gone, as was most of the back of his head. The pilothouse was sticky with blood and brains.

Lipardo swore vengeance. It wasn't so much a matter of friendship, although he had thought well of Snake. It was a matter of taking blood for blood.

The intercom light was blinking. Lipardo reached for it.

"Hello, Lipardo in the pilothouse."

It was Gurrola. His second-in-command described the situation and his proposed tactics.

"Good. Shall I have the engines started?"

"Yes. If we can't shoot the bastard, maybe we can ram him. I'd like to get the body, though."

"You think it's the Executioner?"

"If it isn't, there's somebody else around just as dangerous."

"You have a point—" Gurrola began.

Lipardo didn't listen. He heard something else, a distant rumble and roar, growing rapidly louder and closer. Forgetting for a moment where he was, he half rose.

A bullet snapped by his head, taking out another pilothouse window and nearly taking his head with it. Lipardo ducked, sweating. He'd seen enough.

There was a flaw in his plan, after all.

"Danny? Danny?" Gurrola shouted from the intercom.

"Get underway right now," Lipardo yelled. "And get all the ARs up on deck, too. Our sniper has friends, and they're coming fast!"

GUZMAN WAS HURRYING AFT, his Blackhawk drawn. With Bolan on the job, confusion reigned aboard *Sirena*.

Lipardo and Gurrola were doing their best to get things sorted out. Given five minutes, they might succeed. Bolan probably wasn't going to give them that much time. Even if he did, five minutes was enough to get Angelita free. Or at least get between her and anyone sent down with orders to kill her.

It might be the end of both his cover and his life, but he was the man on the spot, and he had to help Angelita. He'd rather be dead himself than have her on his conscience.

The cabin was locked from the outside, but with a bolt, not a key. Guzman yanked the bolt back, to find Angelita unbound and crouched in a corner with the table lamp in her hand, ready to swing it at Guzman's skull.

"Fredo!"

"Good thing you recognized me. I don't have my badge handy—"

"What's this about a badge?" came a voice from behind him.

Guzman didn't turn. He knew what that would do, with Vennera having the drop on him.

"I thought you might be a problem, but I didn't think you might be a cop. Now, drop your gun." The Blackhawk hit the rug.

"Both of you over where I can see you."

Angelita cringed and dropped the lamp. Guzman had to look twice before he realized the cringing was an act.

"Please—"

"If you beg, I'll kill you slowly. Move!"

Angelita moved—faster than Guzman thought he could.

"Slowly!" Vennera hissed.

Angelita was now almost glacial as she moved toward the bulkhead. As she reached it, she seemed to stagger, then spread-eagle herself against the wall and slowly flow down into a heap on the floor.

Vennera froze for one vital second. He also took his eyes off Guzman.

The undercover cop flung himself on the man, slamming him against the wall with all his two hundred pounds. He chopped at Vennera's wrist, sending his Colt Python flying.

The hardman's hand darted for his pocket.

"Look out!" Angelita shouted.

Guzman whirled and saw Jorge Langas and two gunners in the corridor, gaping, not yet drawing. They looked as if they couldn't believe what they saw.

Guzman had no such problem. He had his holdout gun clear of its ankle strap before the first gunner had his weapon clear of leather. At ten feet he put four rounds into the three men.

Another string of shots rang out behind him. He spun around to see Angelita and Vennera lying in a bloody mess on the floor. Then Angelita rolled clear, the hardman's Colt in both hands.

Vennera didn't move, and a close look told Guzman why. Angelita had put the muzzle of the man's gun against his ear before she fired.

CARLOS LUNA DUCKED AS the rifle bursts swarmed overhead.

"Lousy shooting," Sergeant Abas observed.

"Let's not give them a chance to get better." Luna cut the throttles to the port and center engines and threw the helm over. Starboard engine and rudder together swung the cruiser in a tight turn.

"Hey, they're getting underway," Abas said.

Luna swore. Water bubbled, then foamed at *Sirena*'s stern. A faint curl of bow wave appeared.

"Let's swing around and get Bolan out of the water," Abas suggested. "When those charges blow—"

The lake erupted under the yacht's stern. A curtain of water fifty feet high shot into the air, hiding the vessel all the way forward to her streamlined funnel. Bits and pieces of metal and at least one complete human body rose with the curtain.

As the charges went off, the riflemen on the upper deck got the cruiser's range. But the blast ruined their aim. Instead of spraying the cockpit and butchering the two men, they sprayed the hull.

That was bad enough. Bullets ripped into the un-protected extra gasoline tanks, pouring high-octane gasoline into the bilges. The engines' ignitions did the rest.

Flames boomed up from aft, sweeping forward. Luna tossed the raft on the bow over the side, then slapped Abas.

"Move!"

"What—"

Luna spun the wheel over. Incredibly at least one engine was still running in the middle of the flames. Now the boat was pointed directly at the yacht.

The riflemen opened up again as they saw the cruiser bearing down on them. Their aims were way off, but they were putting out a lot of lead.

Carlos Luna felt a bullet sear his shoulder as he went over the side. He also heard a hiss as he struck the water. The flames must have reached his clothes; well, a whole lakeful of cold water would keep down any burns.

The cruiser's engines didn't die until she rammed *Sirena* amidships, although the riflemen were firing at her all the way. As Luna started swimming cau-tiously, head low, he noticed that the yacht was listing by the stern.

MACK BOLAN WAS CAREFUL TO stay out of the water until the charges went off. From the size of the blast, he suspected that both of them had gone off together. If he'd been in the water, he'd have been gutted like a lake trout.

Now he was swimming twenty feet down, the Be-retta in its waterproof container, the grenades in another. He'd taken a sight on the boarding ladder and knew where to come up. The yacht was no longer under power, and she couldn't drift very fast.

She could catch fire, though, and that might be the last straw for the prisoners.

The vessel's hull loomed above Bolan. He rolled over on his back to study the mangled plates of her stern. It would be a race between fire and water.

The boarding ladder was still there, however. The warrior dived, then finned rapidly upward. As his head broke water, he flung himself at the highest rung he could reach.

DANNY LIPARDO HADN'T heard any shots from the sniper since the cruiser had rammed *Sirena*. Maybe they'd got him.

Maybe, but he'd done enough damage. Three men down besides Snake, and everybody having to keep covered from both sides. If the riflemen hadn't been afraid of being shot in the back, maybe they could have stopped those crazies in the sports cruiser.

And all hell was breaking loose below decks. The engines were off their mountings, the stern was leaking and some bastard had barricaded himself and Angelita in the bow. He'd shot Langas, who was no big loss, and a couple of soldiers who were.

Well, if he just stayed there long enough, that problem would solve itself. He, the yacht and the Lirio woman would all go to the bottom of the lake together.

If only Vennera would show up! Right now the little man would look like the cavalry coming to the rescue. If he went into action, he would eat Angelita raw for breakfast, and Lipardo would hand him the salt.

Lipardo popped a fresh magazine into his AR-15 and looked back at Gurrola. The chief was squatting on the deck, keeping his head down at least. The Hi-Power was in his hand, but he had the sense not to join the firefight.

Somebody shouted from aft, then somebody screamed. Lipardo heard bursts from both AR-15s and pistols and swung around, looking aft.

As he did, a bow window of the pilothouse exploded. A piece of glass gouged Gurrola's cheek. He wiped away the blood with his free hand and frowned.

"Danny, I think this is getting out of hand."

BOLAN HAD REACHED THE YACHT'S main deck undetected, but he had to take out two men in the main saloon. The gunshots alerted the surviving riflemen on the upper deck, so they were alert when he climbed up. They also started with the edge in firepower.

Their alertness and firepower didn't make as much difference as they might have. For one thing, they were facing the Executioner. For another, they knew they were on a sinking ship. Some of them already had begun to think of imitating rats, which didn't help their marksmanship.

Bolan took out two of the four men in 3-round bursts from the Beretta. The others drove him to cover. He also saw that the pilothouse still had life in it, life with another AR-15.

That was the moment somebody forward shot out the pilothouse windows. Bolan saw the surviving riflemen looking over their shoulders and rose to pull the pin on a grenade, and let the explosive fly.

LIPARDO HAD JUST KNOCKED out an aft-facing pilot-house window when the grenade sailed through.

It took him all of half a second to recognize what the object was. That left him two seconds to pick a window that might be out of the attacker's line of sight and dive through it.

He'd just hit the deck outside when the grenade exploded. Hector Gurrola died without a chance to scream, feel pain, or even be outraged at his underling's treachery.

Lipardo kept on rolling, through the railing and into the water. He let himself sink a long way before he started swimming. Even when he broke the surface, he did it only long enough to fill his lungs.

The fight on the yacht should last long enough to keep the Executioner from pursuing him, or even noticing that he was gone. If it did, Lipardo wasn't finished yet.

He'd need a head start and half a dozen men, from Gurrola's gang or any other, who would remain loyal to him. That wasn't much, but drug lords more powerful than Gurrola had often started with less.

The water was cold, but the thought of his next battle against the Executioner kept Lipardo warm all the way to shore.

ONE OF THE RIFLEMEN SHOT a wild burst at Bolan when the warrior launched the grenade. He took him out of play with the Beretta, then he threw another grenade, which blew one of the riflemen apart and the other off the upper deck. He landed on his head and didn't move again.

One last man on the upper deck made a break for it. Bolan was reloading when he did, and the man might have got away. Except that Fredo Guzman and Angelita came around the forward end of the superstructure at that moment. They were both armed, and both of them fired. Enough bullets and shotgun slugs slammed into the hardman to not only kill him but to knock him over the side.

Bolan dropped to the main deck in front of the new arrivals. Guzman looked unusually sober, and Angelita looked ten years older. Then he saw blood all over her clothing.

"Angelita—"

"It's not mine," she said. "I—I didn't feel like—skinny-dipping. But all the clothes around—we'd shot the people—the people—" She swallowed and put out a hand.

Bolan let her grip his without pulling her closer. After a moment she swallowed again, put down her shotgun, then nodded.

"Okay, I think."

"Can you swim to shore?"

"Never mind," Guzman said, pointing over the side. The cabin cruiser was gliding toward *Sirena*, steering erratically. Bolan looked closer and recognized Sergeant Abas at the wheel.

He cupped his hands. "Where's Carlos?"

"He took a bullet and got his hair and clothes on fire, before we bailed out," the sergeant called back. "He'll be okay if we can get him to a hospital."

Under Bolan's feet, the yacht lurched. He saw the bow begin to swing upward and black smoke pour up from below.

"People, if that's not the fuel tanks catching fire, I don't want to wait around and find out what it is," he said. "Is Dino...?"

Guzman jerked a thumb over the side. "Last night."

Bolan shrugged. Rough justice, but Dino didn't have any kids, and his wife would be taken care of. Bolan would make sure that Salvador Lirio remembered that obligation if the old man managed to forget it.

He looked at Angelita. "Will 'ladies first' insult you, Captain Lirio?"

"Under the circumstances, no." Moving stiffly, she swung herself over the railing and dropped onto the deck of the cabin cruiser.

In a minute the others followed. In another ten minutes they looked astern to see the yacht vanish, leaving only a cloud of smoke and some bobbing wreckage. The sports cruiser burned for a bit longer, but she, too, was on the bottom before they were out of sight.

17

Salvador Lirio sat in the breakfast nook of the house where he'd first met Milo Bruning, and sipped coffee. The morning *Chicago Tribune* lay unread on the table in front of him.

The house wasn't really safe, of course. For Salvador Lirio there was no such thing in Chicago, probably in the Midwest, probably even in the whole United States. So he'd fled only to this house in the suburbs, where his family would be safe from the men who would come for him sooner or later.

Or at least safer. There would be others, possibly from Gurrola's little army, certainly from other gangs, who would come to his house. But if no one there knew anything and no one was a witness to his kidnapping, there would be less danger for them.

By stepping forward to face Gurrola's men alone, Lirio had bought time for his family and servants. Time that Milo Bruning would use very well.

A knock rattled the door.

"Come in," Lirio said. "The door isn't locked."

They came in. There were four of them, and he recognized three but gave no sign of it.

"You are coming with us, old man," one with a thick mustache said.

"What, no 'Don Salvador'?" Lirio asked. "I didn't think Don Hector was served by men with so little—"

One of the men stepped forward and slapped him across the face. His head rocked back, and he tasted blood from his bitten tongue.

"Ah," was all Lirio said. He saw the mustached man glaring at the one who'd slapped him. At some other time it might be worth the risk. Provoking one of the hot-tempered ones into hurting him would divide the four men. Doubtless the leader had orders from Don Hector—or more likely, from Danny Lipardo—to bring the old man in alive.

But if he was unconscious, they might think of searching him. Then they would find some things they might not otherwise even look for, because who would expect an old man like Salvador Lirio to have them?

Slowly, keeping his hands in plain sight, Salvador Lirio stood up. "I presume you are aware that I need insulin daily?"

"We have as much as you're likely to need," the mustached man said. He pulled a pair of handcuffs out of one jacket pocket. From the bulge in the other, Liro judged it held a gun, and another bulge under the jacket was probably a second gun in a shoulder holster. The other men looked equally well-armed.

Lirio nodded and held out his hands for the cuffs

SEVERAL HOURS ELAPSED before Bolan learned of Salvador Lirio's disappearance. He was sure that he knew what had happened, but he couldn't just rush off on Lirio's trail, rescue the old man and finish off Gurrola's survivors.

There was Carlos Luna to get into a hospital and doctors to keep from asking too many questions, the Coast Guard to confuse about what had happened to *Sirena* and Justice Department agents to brief, hastily flown in from Chicago on orders from Hal Brognola.

There should have been Angelita Lirio to see into the hospital, too, but she threatened to use Vennera's Colt on Bolan if he made an issue of it. She went into the outpatient clinic, had her worst cuts and burns looked at, then started drawing a map of the Lirio estate for Bolan.

She'd finished the map when she met Bolan and Fredo Guzman in the hospital coffee shop. The warrior studied it, and pointed to a pair of dotted lines ending halfway across the rear lawn.

"A tunnel?"

"It should be. It leads from the fallout shelter to an emergency exit."

Bolan nodded. Any route to the fallout shelter also led to the pistol range, where Gurrola's arsenal was located. From the pistol range, it was also possible to penetrate the main house. If the attack drew the remaining hardmen down into the basement, so much the better. There'd be no family or servants in the line of fire.

"Aren't we getting a bit ahead of ourselves?" Fredo Guzman complained. "What's to prove there's anybody left from any gang at the estate?"

"What's to prove there isn't?" Angelita demanded.

"It's going to mean splitting our forces," Guzman warned.

"Of course," Bolan agreed. "I'll go back to Chicago and check out the house. If there's anybody there we need to take out, I'm the best man for the job.

"Fredo, you keep the Lirio lodge under surveillance, you and anybody Justice can spare from guarding Carlos. Keep your distance, though. If you spook them into moving Lirio, you might want to think about a new job in Zanzibar."

"You can't—" Guzman began.

"Captain Gallery can. If the Lirio family and the Justice Department both ask him to, he will."

Guzman shrugged. "Okay. But why the hell should they show up at the lodge?"

"They'll already have people in place there," Angelita said. "Maybe informants on the local police or sheriff's office. Also, it's easily defensible, or so they think."

"They're right, too," Guzman said. "One dipshit little road up to the lodge, and cliffs on all the other sides. Nobody's going to get in there without being seen unless they fly."

Angelita grinned. "Have you forgotten that I fly helicopters for a living? I've got ratings in a few kinds of fixed-wing planes, too."

Guzman actually looked embarrassed. "Hey, I guess I shot my mouth off again. It's still going to be hairy, though."

"If it was easy, it wouldn't be half as much fun," Angelita replied.

"Let's worry about the fun later," Bolan said, folding the map and stuffing it inside his windbreaker. "Angelita, can you give me some sort of message that will make the family trust me? If I have to break in shooting, they might just decide I'm another hardman."

"I'll record something on a cassette. But I thought I was coming—"

Bolan held up a hand. Angelita frowned. She would be glaring in another minute. Bolan decided to address the soldier rather than the woman or granddaughter.

"Captain, I'm not saying I wouldn't rather have you along. But right now we have a real advantage. Lipardo probably doesn't know that you're alive. Your piloting skills and your knowledge of the Lirio house are assets he won't expect us to have. The longer we keep you up our sleeves, the better our chances of taking the pot."

"I always did think Hector Gurrola cheated at poker," Angelita said, scratching at a burn on her chin. "I won't mind being your hole card if that's the way you want it. Just as long as I'm in at the finish."

"I can practically guarantee that," Bolan assured her. He lowered his voice. "I want you to charter a fixed-wing plane here while I check out helicopters for charter in Wisconsin. Then I want you to fly me down to Wisconsin and wait while I go to Chicago. I'll join you as soon as I can, and we'll take the chopper north to surprise the lodge."

"Where in Wisconsin?" was Angelita's only question.

"Ideally some place where the helicopter can reach the lodge in a single hop. That'll give us a better chance of surprise."

A TERRIFIC SNEEZE SPOILED the dignity of Danny Lipardo's greeting to Don Salvador Lirio. He blew his nose and held out his hand.

The old man would have stepped back if two hard-men hadn't held his shoulders. He could still leave his hands dangling in their cuffs in front of him.

"Don Salvador, you reject my hospitality. That isn't the act of a gentleman."

"Little man," Don Salvador said, seeming to look down at Lipardo from a great height. "You do not offer a man the hospitality of his own property. As for being a gentleman—a mark of being one is to know those who are not."

Lipardo's curse turned into a cough. When the coughing spell had passed, he jerked a hand toward the door of the lodge.

"Take him to his room. Take off the handcuffs, give him what he wants to eat and drink. Let him wash if he insists."

The mustached man made a hand signal to Lipardo.

The gang chief shook his head. Drugs could keep a prisoner docile or make him talkative. But when the prisoner was eighty-four, diabetic and had to be kept alive, they were also too risky.

Don Salvador and his escorts disappeared inside the log-walled lodge. Lipardo decided that a brief walk might ease the grip the cold had on his chest and throat.

It didn't, but a fresh look at the gang's refuge was almost as good. The lodge itself had log walls that could resist grenades, except where it had stone walls that could stand off artillery. It was stocked with a month's supply of food and water.

Cliffs surrounded the area on three sides, nearly vertical except where they actually overhung the forest below. Dense second-growth pine grew right up to the base of the cliffs, except by the beaver pond. There the ground was oozy mud, not real quicksand but just about as hard to get through.

Lipardo pulled a package of tissues and a notebook out of his coat pocket. He blew his nose, then jotted down two places that gave a good field of fire on the road. He had twelve men with him, and at any moment four of them would be alert and armed with automatic weapons.

He'd have five more men and some long-range hunting rifles when the party he'd sent out returned tonight. That was a risk, but it was one he had to run in order to get the extra firepower. This wasn't the city, where a man could be blown away at fifty yards or so. Here you had to be able to see and hit a man a quarter-mile off.

This wasn't Lipardo's home turf, and he didn't like it. But it was fight here or just give up, flee without a friend to guard his back and start over again somewhere else with no resources and a lot of enemies. He'd be better off dead, which wouldn't take long, either.

As it was, he'd have seventeen men when the foraging party returned. Enough to hold the hill, but not too many to take with him when Salvador Lirio paid the price they'd ask for the old man's life. When they were across the border, seventeen was also a good number for starting over. Enough for muscle, not too many to pay with Lirio's money until something else turned up to bring in the dollars.

Pine tops danced in a rising wind, and Lipardo felt a sneeze coming on. He turned his back to the wind and walked back toward the lodge.

18

Captain Gallery needed answers, and he needed them now. He wasn't used to being kept in the dark, and he'd had enough. Questions twisted his guts—what was Carlos Luna doing in a hospital in the upper peninsula, and where was Fredo Guzman? Maybe the number he was dialing would give him satisfaction.

A recorded, rather wimpy voice told Gallery that if he was inquiring about his account balance, to press One. If he wanted to talk about anything else, or didn't have a touch-tone phone . . .

Gallery followed his instructions and savagely punched One. A lot of clicking and buzzing sounded on the line.

Then a surprisingly familiar voice came on the line.

"Captain Gallery?"

"Who's this?"

"The man with the information you wanted."

"Okay."

"Is that all you've got to say, Captain?"

"No way, mister. What was Carlos Luna hunting when he got into that hunting accident? And where's Sergeant Guzman?"

"You heard of a yacht sinking up north?"

"*Sirena*, the Lirios' boat?"

"That's the one."

"That was Carlos's hunting accident?"

"Give the man a teddy bear."

Gallery decided that Brognola was either under more strain than usual or was even more of a smart-ass than before, or both. He also decided to ignore bad manners to get hard Intelligence.

"Is the case closed out?"

"No."

"So if I guessed that Fredo was still working on it—"

"You'd guess the reason why we don't want you to pull him in."

"What does 'we' mean, Federal man?"

"Me and some friends. They include the President of the United States, if you don't mind my dropping names. They also include a man who's saved us all a lot of trouble with bad guys we couldn't touch legally."

Short of an engraved plaque, that was about as close to an ID on the Executioner as Gallery had ever got.

"So you don't want me to touch him or anybody working with him?"

"Is the Pope a Catholic?"

"I never argue religion, politics or women. Just make sure that Fredo turns up, dead or alive, before I have to start bullshitting the Violent Crimes commander. He isn't going to like that. He might even take a dislike to working with you in the future."

"Understood," came the voice on the line. "How long is that?"

"Three, four more days."

"No sweat. Our friend has an extra job to tackle before he joins Fredo, but it's a quickie."

"Anybody we know?"

"How about the Vitellis?"

A click, and there was nothing but buzzing in Gallery's ears. He hung up, praying that he'd just been told the truth.

He didn't bother with any other prayers. The Executioner didn't need them.

MACK BOLAN WISHED HE had some hard Intel. Had Danny Lipardo left some of his own people in the Lirio mansion? Or was the occupying force strictly Vitelli and Langas soldiers, and maybe a few others scraped up off the streets?

If the Vitellis were running the show, it meant they and Lipardo weren't exactly friends anymore. Optimistically speaking, it also meant that the estate's security system would be in the hands of people still learning how to operate it.

Bolan unwound a rope with a grappling hook attached, swung it a few times, then let it fly toward an overhanging oak branch. The hook caught and held on the second attempt. The warrior climbed into the tree, then lay flat on the branch to study the estate. A light ground fog would cut visibility both ways. He also saw that Angelita was right. Since the time when the rear entrance to the fallout shelter had been built, the bushes and trees between it and the house had grown. Now they were twice or even three times the height of a man.

Once Bolan got to the entrance, he'd be invisible from the house. Then all he had to do was cope with any defenses Gurrola might have put in the tunnel.

One headache at a time. Bolan pulled up the rope, crawled to the trunk and dropped soundlessly onto damp, straggly grass matted with last fall's dead leaves. He made his way toward the entrance, easily staying out of the lights. He reached the shelter entrance without seeing or hearing any sign of an alarm. The steel door showed a few patches of peeling green paint and a lot of rust, but the chain and padlock were new. Bolan pulled out his bolt cutters and went to work.

Minutes later the warrior had the door open wide enough to admit a slight youth. Then its long-unused hinges gave out a tortured screech.

Bolan froze, the Beretta in hand, until he was sure the noise hadn't alerted security guards. Then he managed to push the door open enough so that he could squeeze through. He took the pack off, placed and wired a surprise he was leaving behind for any pursuers, then pushed the pack through the gap. With the Beretta probing the darkness, he entered the shelter.

Once inside he pulled the door shut and switched on the caver's light hooked to his belt.

The tunnel showed no signs of being used lately. The mud on the floor was thick and free of footprints.

Bolan pulled on his pack and advanced down the tunnel. Fifty feet inside, he was brought up short by the sight of human remains. Some of them were only skeletons with no more than a few shreds of blackened flesh clinging to them. Others were still shrouded in plastic garbage bags, though a couple hadn't been afforded even that dignity. The stench in the confines of the tunnel was almost unbearable.

The warrior stepped carefully past the bodies, to find the roof of the tunnel brushing his hair. He crouched and shone the light ahead. Another thirty feet down the tunnel, and the roof had sagged halfway to the floor. From the fresh dirt and mortar on the floor, this was recent.

Bolan had never been a tunnel rat in Vietnam. He was much too big. But he'd learned the basic techniques of underground work, because he knew they might someday save his life. He'd been right, too.

He unslung his pack and tied the rope to it, then hooked the rope to his belt and got down on hands and knees. He made twenty feet past the beginning of the sag before the roof bumped the top of his head. A chunk of mortar popped loose and crept under the neck of the blacksuit.

Bolan went flat on his belly, pulled the mortar out and stuck it into the mud. Then he began a low crawl, light in his teeth, Beretta in one hand, and knees and feet doing most of the work.

How long he crawled and how low the ceiling came, he never quite knew. He felt mortar falling at least twice, and once he heard something that sounded like the beginning of a rockfall, but it didn't go on.

Three times he crawled over what were unmistakably human bones. The third time, he also felt the ceiling brushing his hair again, even though his chin was leaving a trail in the mud.

The warrior slowed his crawl even more, reaching into the twilight with the delicate touch of a watchmaker. If anything shifted now...

After a long time when he hardly dared to breathe, he felt the ceiling rise clear of his head. A moment later he could roll over and shine the light six feet straight up.

Ahead a faint square of light traced itself in the darkness. The lights in the pistol range were creeping around the edge of the door at the far end of the tunnel, no more than another fifty feet.

Bolan squatted and inched his pack through the tight space. Once it caught on something, probably human remains, and tugging only strained the rope. He was beginning to be afraid he'd have to crawl back and free it by hand when the object holding it back pulled out of the mud. The pack slid out, covered with mud and mortar. Bolan brushed everything off as well as he could, then checked his weapons.

He did that with his back turned to the door, shrouding the light with his body. He'd heard voices in the pistol range. As he chambered a round in the Desert Eagle, he heard pistols cracking. That told him that whoever was down here wasn't a Lirio relative or servant. He could come out shooting.

He could also take a little more time here, leaving another surprise for anyone trying to get out through the tunnel. In two minutes he'd wired a charge powerful enough to kill anyone who set it off and bring the roof down on top of anyone with him.

The door was locked from the inside, and Bolan faced another tactical decision. He could blow the lock, but at the risk of knocking himself out with the concussion and maybe collapsing the tunnel, as well. He could also go slow, at the risk of still doing noisy work when the gunners on the range were through practicing and able to hear him.

Fortunately the light seeping around the door let him study it without turning on his own belt light. It showed him rusted hinges, one with the bolt almost gone, and mortar crumbling around both of them.

The bolt cutters took care of the first hinge. Two minutes' judicious gouging with the point of a Gerber knife took care of the mortar. With the door held in place by its own weight, Bolan drew the Uzi, fed a tape-and-turn pair of magazines into it, then rolled onto his back.

As he rolled forward, combat boots with steel plates in the soles crashed into the door, which rang like an ancient and out-of-tune bell. The hinges squealed.

The chatter in the pistol range stopped abruptly. Bolan flipped the Uzi selector to full-auto and kicked the door again.

The weight of the steel was too much for the lock. It twisted with a scream, the door sagged and Bolan kicked it again. As the door toppled, he rolled upright, spraying 9 mm bullets into the room and the two men facing him.

They'd have time to turn, and one had time to draw. Then their time ran out as the Executioner's 9 mm punch slammed them backward.

Bolan leaped into the room, whirling to face the door. Nobody came through before he reached it and threw the bolt.

Maybe he hadn't even alerted anyone outside the range. It was the one place in the house where the sound of gunfire was normal.

The Executioner decided he'd won himself a little extra time, and began a quick search of the range. He found what he was looking for—the household arsenal: AR-15s, Uzis, a couple of Ingrams, CS grenades and even a few black-powder weapons that must have belonged to some Gurrola soldier with a weakness for antiques. Not to mention enough ammunition to keep all of them shooting for much too long.

If the soldiers in the house had to rely on what they were packing when Bolan hit, things were looking up. The warrior hadn't expected to lose, but he'd been worried about innocent casualties. A firefight in the Lirio house was something he'd been determined to avoid, but when the Vitellis had moved in, he'd been forced to make the best of a bad job. Now that best might just be good enough.

Bolan was wiring a charge to the gun cabinet when he heard fists pounding on the door.

"Hey, in there! Didn't you hear the phone?"

"What phone?" Bolan shouted. "Damned if I heard a thing!" He looked around and saw that he'd accidentally wiped out the intercom along with the two hitters.

"Well, get your ass in gear, Tomasso. Somebody's been screwing around with the old fallout-shelter entrance. We think they might be hiding in the tunnel."

"Haven't heard anything," Bolan said, slipping toward the door. "Want me to check it out or come up?"

"I'll come on in. You, me and Manny, we oughta be enough to sit on the guns—"

Bolan jerked the door open, thrust the Uzi into the stomach of the man outside and fired. The hardman was dead before he could even stagger. He toppled against the man behind him, spoiling his draw. Bolan's next burst removed most of the second man's head, from the eyebrows.

A third man on the stairs spent a half second too long gaping at the Executioner. Bolan ran the second magazine dry killing him, then dropped both and slammed in a fresh pair. With sixty 9 mm rounds waiting in the Uzi, he took a position where he could see the whole staircase. Nobody was going to get a shot at Bolan without his shooting first. Grenades might be a problem, but he was between the hardmen and their arsenal.

Instead of more men, a shout floated down the stairs.

"What the hell's going on down there?"

Bolan pitched his voice to sound panicky. "Somebody's come in through the tunnel. Tomasso's dead, and I don't see Manny. I'm pinned."

The warrior let off a 3-round burst, then screamed in a convincing imitation of a wounded man.

He heard cursing at the top of the stairs. Somebody muttered, "Dumb asshole getting himself wasted. Isn't it enough we got half the men tied down keeping the family in their rooms?"

Bolan ended the man's complaining by launching himself up the stairs, firing on the run. Three men on the landing caught the hailstorm of 9 mm lead. One flew backward, smashing into an antique table, turning it to kindling wood as he fell. A second dived down the stairs, landing apparently unhurt and rolling toward the door of the pistol range.

The third man ran for his life. Bolan aimed low and cut his legs out from under him. Then the Uzi rose to take out a man who'd just stepped off the stairs to the second floor. It rose a little too far; 9 mm slugs ripped plaster and a chandelier from the ceiling.

Salvador Lirio was going to be hiring decorators as well as shipbuilders when this was over. Somehow Bolan didn't think the man would complain. It was better than hiring lawyers—or having his relatives hire undertakers.

Bolan wanted to press his advantage, but knew he couldn't leave the man who'd fallen downstairs at his back. Even if the man didn't join the shooting, he could warn the gunners who'd gone out to check the shelter entrance.

Bolan bounded down the stairs and reached the bottom just as the hardman found the gun cabinet. Suddenly the warrior found himself going back up the stairs, propelled by the explosion.

Everything must have gone up together, HE, black powder, propellants and the rest of the arsenal. Bolan's ears rang, his teeth were gritty with plaster dust, powder and mortar. He had to lean against a wall for a moment.

Then a long rumble cut through the ringing in his ears, the unmistakable sound of the tunnel collapsing. It went on and on, more dust poured up from the basement and the bodies at the foot of the stairs vanished in the murk.

Bolan hoped that the shelter's collapsing wouldn't undermine the foundations of the house.

He would have to move even faster than before, or all his efforts to keep the Lirios clear of police attention would be wasted. It would be too much to hope that the explosion hadn't been heard outside the confines of the estate.

A nightmare figure clad in black cloth and gray dust, the Executioner stalked through the halls of the Lirio mansion. His first stop was the music room, where he found two hardmen. One of them had a radio. Bolan saw that they were looking out across the rear lawn, and guessed they were the link with the men at the tunnel entrance.

He gave them a reprieve. He wanted the men out back to think that everything was normal until one of them tripped a certain wire.

Bolan used the back stairs, which rose from the mud room into the servants' quarters. He passed a small window halfway up. As he did, white light blazed out on the rear lawn.

A moment later he heard the crash of an explosion and the screams of injured men. The window shivered and cracked, and all the lights went out.

Quite a few people, men and women both, started cursing or praying in Spanish. A man shouted in English, "Jesus Christ, what the hell's going on out there tonight?"

It was unfortunate for the man to have called out— he'd given away his position, right at the top of the stairs. He was the next to die, but he wasn't the last. Others followed in rapid succession. They were leaderless, confused, frightened and didn't know if someone looming up in the dark hall was friend or foe. Bolan had no such problem, and the gang's rearguard was down in less than five minutes.

He fired his last shots of the night at the men in the music room. One of them went down; the other plunged through the French windows without bothering to open them. He ran a few steps before collapsing on the patio, his severed jugular pumping blood onto the flagstones.

Bolan was reloading his Uzi when he heard footsteps behind him. He whirled, drawing the Desert Eagle, but stopped short of squeezing the trigger.

One of Lirio's servants faced him, a man at least sixty and nearly bald. But his hands were large and firm, and so was their grip on a Colt Chief's model picked up from one of the hardmen. Behind him was a large woman, holding an absurdly small .22, some dead hardman's holdout gun.

Bolan spoke in Spanish. "I mean no harm to the Lirio family or their servants. So you can put your guns away."

"Ha!" the woman said. The man remained silent.

Bolan tried again. "I have a tape from Dona Angelita, to explain who—"

"You may explain to the police," the man interrupted. "Now, you'll put your gun not away, but on the floor. Then you'll get down—"

"Nicholas. Ramona. What is this?"

This voice was soft but carried the weight of both years and authority. Bolan looked up the stairs as the two servants whirled.

Elena Lirio stood at the head of the stairs, wearing a dark red dressing gown and leaning on a cane.

"This man—" Nicholas began.

"This man might have saved us all tonight. If you fools don't shoot him or force him to shoot you, he might save Don Salvador. Have you thought of that? Have you, in fact, thought at all?"

As she spoke, Dona Elena made her way down the stairs. Each step was an effort, but the two servants were too surprised to help her. It was Bolan who met her halfway and helped her to a chair in the music room.

She brushed glass from the French window off the upholstery, threw a disgusted look at the dead hardman and held out her hand.

"You spoke of a tape?"

"Yes."

"Ramona, bring the cassette player from Teresa's room. It may redeem itself finally by playing something besides that loud rock music. Nicholas, start organizing the men to find light and clear away these bodies."

"Dona Elena, I have my own player, and time is important. If I'm here when the police arrive, it might delay rescuing your husband."

The Lirio matriarch looked at Bolan. "They won't hold you, surely?"

"I wouldn't doubt it."

"Very well."

Bolan handed over the miniature player with its tape. Dona Elena listened to it, then blinked away tears.

"You seem to have won Angelita's loyalty. Go and finish your work."

"Thank you. It wouldn't be a bad idea to arm some of your more reliable servants and have them search the grounds. Not all of your enemies may be dead or on the run."

"It shall be as you wish. Nicholas, start picking the veterans. Go with God."

"The same to you."

Bolan turned away and began collecting his weapons. He would have liked to stay and make sure that trigger-happy servants groping in the darkness didn't blow one another away, but he had just enough time to reach the little Wisconsin airport where Angelita waited if he crowded the speed limit every mile of the way.

The Vitellis had shot themselves dry. The same couldn't be said about Danny Lipardo.

19

Danny Lipardo was worried about two things—one was his cold turning to bronchitis or even pneumonia, and the other was that his men weren't back yet with the supply truck. He'd expected them mid-afternoon, within hours after their coded phone call signaled that they'd found the food and weapons. He'd thought that they might have been caught, or at least tailed and forced to hide.

Now he was beginning to think that they'd simply got lost on the winding, treacherous back roads. If they had any sense, they'd probably stop for the night as soon as the light failed. Otherwise they'd risk missing a turn and ending up burning among the trees at the bottom of a cliff.

Of course, if it wasn't for the food and hunting rifles the truck was carrying, Lipardo wouldn't have cared much whether the men returned or not. Salvador Lirio didn't seem to object to a five-million-dollar price on his life. Five million dollars for twelve men was a better stake than the same amount for seventeen.

The only virtue of this place was that it was impenetrable. Not even the Executioner could touch him.

BY THE TIME THE BELL JetRanger was ten miles from the lodge, Mack Bolan was quite sure that Angelita Lirio was a frustrated gunship pilot. She liked to fly so low that Bolan looked up at the tops of tall rocks, never mind trees. Faced with an obstacle, she would pull up at the last moment, slide over it, then drop down on the other side.

The last obstacle was a rocky hilltop. Angelita dropped the machine into a clear-cut patch of hillside, neatly avoiding boulders and stumps. She cut the engine back to idle while Bolan made a final check of his equipment.

"How's our fuel?" he asked when he'd completed the check.

"Normal or even a bit more than that. Maybe we didn't need that overload tank after all."

"Better safe than sorry. If we can't make the rendezvous with Fredo, we may need to fly a little farther than we'd planned."

"To get out of Lipardo's reach?"

"Right. I don't plan to leave him or any of his people in shape to chase us. But my primary objective is pulling your grandfather out of there. If that means leaving Lipardo and his people to the Justice Department—"

"If I know my grandfather, the first thing he's going to say if we do that is to insist you go back and finish the job. He's likely to take being kidnapped kind of personally."

"I won't argue with him, as long as he stays behind." Bolan looked at his watch. "Let's make it straight in as fast as we can go. From here on out, we'll be close enough for them to hear us at any speed or altitude. Our best chance is to hit them before they realize what's happening."

"No sweat."

The rotors swung slowly, then blurred as Angelita fed in more power. Her bandaged hands danced over controls, and the JetRanger shot up out of the clearing like a rocket. She caught it just above the treetops, checked the course to the lodge on the compass, then opened the throttle.

The next three minutes were like riding a dragon. Treetops whipped past inches below the skids. Sometimes the helicopter tilted suddenly as Angelita banked to avoid a tree taller than its fellows. Bolan seldom saw the trees before Angelita took evasive action; he concluded that she had superb night vision.

"One minute," she shouted in his ear. She cut power as Bolan slid the door open and tightened his harness.

"Thirty seconds." Now Bolan could see the hill looming ahead. He could even see a spark of light from a window in the lodge. Or had Lipardo mounted searchlights? Bolan tensed, partly for his leap, partly to pull Angelita clear if tracer bullets suddenly ripped into the JetRanger.

Angelita brought the helicopter around in a wide sweeping turn, ending up at the base of the cliff. Then she opened the throttle again. They shot up three hundred feet in a matter of seconds.

As the top of the cliff approached, Bolan crouched in the open door. As it appeared, he flung himself outward, waiting for the jarring thud that would tell him he'd judged his leap correctly. If it didn't come, he'd be facing a three-hundred-foot fall....

The rocky soil slammed into his knees and ribs. He rode the shock with a paratrooper's five-point roll, taking only minor bruises from his equipment. As he rose to hands and knees, he saw the helicopter soar above the roof of the lodge, then sink as rapidly as it had climbed.

The plan was for Angelita to evade at low altitude and wait in the clearing until Bolan signaled that he'd secured her grandfather. It might take two minutes, or it might take ten.

If it took more than ten, odds were that Bolan and Don Salvador were going to be pinned down by Lipardo's numbers and firepower. Then the warrior only hoped that Angelita wouldn't decide that playing kamikaze would help her grandfather. At close range even pistol bullets could take down a helicopter.

The Beretta was in Bolan's hand as he rose. He had all the time he needed to draw down on the two guards who dashed around the corner of the lodge. One had an Ingram in his hand, but not in firing position.

He never had a chance to raise it, as the Executioner swept the men with quick 3-round bursts. The gunner with the Ingram lurched sideways, slipped on the wet grass as his knees buckled and went over the edge of the cliff. He'd just begun to scream when he struck the ground far below.

The other guard had courage enough to try to draw, even as Bolan loomed over him. The warrior knelt and plucked a stainless-steel .45 out of the man's hand.

"Where's Salvador Lirio?"

"Who...?" The question ended in a bubbling cough and a shake of the head.

"The old man!" Bolan snapped. "Where is he? Answer, or you join your friend."

"Upstairs," the man gasped. "Upstairs. Middle bedroom..." His voice failed as blood trickled from his mouth, but his hand flapped in the general direction of one of the dormer windows.

Bolan saw that it was the only one lighted, and nodded.

The man tried to grip Bolan's hand, but his arm wouldn't obey him. A moment later his breathing stopped. Bolan turned, unwinding his belt rope as he rose. As he started to swing it, he hoped the window frames were as solid as the rest of the lodge seemed to be.

The weighted hook drove through the window with a crash and tinkle of glass. The warrior swarmed up the rope, onto the mist-slick shingles of the roof. He was a sitting duck if anybody came to see what had happened to the guards.

The room beyond the broken window was small, low ceilinged and apparently empty. Or at least the part of it Bolan could see was empty. He cautiously lifted himself onto the top of the dormer so that he could look over the peak of the roof. The open ground beyond the lodge held a garage, a woodshed, three cars and a four-wheel drive vehicle.

The warrior unslung his long-range weapon, an AR-15 retrieved from *Sirena*. All he had to do was blow up a gas tank and it would do a fine job on the vehicles. With their vehicles burning, the men downstairs wouldn't be likely to come upstairs while Bolan was searching the bedrooms.

Bolan knelt on the dormer and sighted on the 4WD, a late-model Cherokee. If he got it burning really nicely, the flames might block the road downhill for at least a few minutes. Long enough for Lipardo's soldiers to think they were trapped, long enough for them to panic.

The rifle cracked, and the slug punched into the Cherokee's tank. The vehicle shivered, shedding glass, then spewed yellow flame.

From below, Bolan heard shouts. He shifted his fire to the next vehicle, something so repainted and customized that it was impossible to tell what it was.

Its gas tank flared, and Bolan slipped back down the roof. As he did, he heard two sharp cracks, shots from a small-caliber revolver.

If he had found Salvador Lirio just a few seconds too late... That thought ended as he swung down from the dormer, feet first through the broken window into the little bedroom.

DANNY LIPARDO WAS GOING upstairs to check on Don Salvador when rifle fire rang out above. Then the Cherokee caught fire, and the man he'd sent to relieve the guards in back found the body of one of them.

Lipardo heard panic in the shouting of his men and fought it down in himself. He forced his feet up the last few steps and down the hall to Lirio's bedroom. He had to secure the old man.

There wasn't going to be any five million dollars. Lipardo and maybe some of his men were going to escape with their lives, if they were lucky. Don Salvador might buy them some luck, if nothing else, and if he couldn't be a pass to safety, he had to be silenced. He knew far too much about Lipardo to be left alive.

"Don Salvador, are you safe?" Lipardo called when he reached the door.

"Of course. These walls are thick enough to stand against anything your rivals are likely to bring. Or do they have antitank guns?"

Lipardo wanted to laugh. So the old man thought this was an attack by a rival gang? He wouldn't say anything to change Lirio's mind. That delusion would make him much more docile, so let him cling to it for as long as he had to live.

Lipardo wanted to kick the door open, but that would spoil his image of a calm man, concerned about Don Salvador's safety. Instead, he unlocked it carefully, drew his Combat Magnum and stepped inside.

He had a moment to realize that Don Salvador was nowhere in sight. He had another moment to start looking.

Then it seemed that an enormous spiked fist punched him in the left eye. That was Danny Lipardo's last sensation, because the .22 slug punched through his eye into his brain.

The accurate range of a Mini-Revolver was about ten feet. Salvador Lirio had fired his holdout gun from less than five feet. He put a second round into Lipardo's temple as the man fell, and checked fire before wasting a third on the dead man.

Then he whirled as a giant black-clad figure seemed to materialize out of the darkness.

BOLAN TOOK IN THE MINI-Revolver in Salvador Lirio's impressively steady hand, the grim look on the old man's face and the sprawled corpse of Danny Lipardo. Instead of drawing his Beretta, he walked over to the body and turned it over with a foot.

"You don't trust my shooting, Mr. Bruning?" Lirio asked, dropping his gun into the pocket of his dressing gown.

"No, Don Salvador. I won't make the same mistake the late Mr. Lipardo made. He certainly didn't have much faith in your shooting." Bolan picked up the Korth Combat Magnum. "Do you think you can handle this?"

Don Salvador hefted the stainless-steel revolver. "Handle it, yes. Hit anything with it, maybe, if I'm lucky enough to have a standing target like Lipardo."

"If you're really lucky, we'll be out of here in a few minutes. How are you at climbing rope ladders?"

"Into helicopters, by any chance?"

"Good guess. Angelita—"

Before Bolan could explain their evacuation route, one of the hardmen loomed in the doorway. He took one look at Lipardo on the floor, another look at Bolan and Don Salvador, then went for his gun.

He'd spent too much time looking before drawing. Both Bolan and Don Salvador fired, and the impact of the bullets slammed the man back out the door, against the railing of the balcony over the living room.

It wasn't as solidly built as it looked; it gave under the weight, and the man crashed to the stone floor below.

From the shouts and shots, Bolan guessed there were no more than two or three men in the living room. He motioned Don Salvador to lie down, then pulled the pin on a CS grenade and tossed it over the railing.

Curses and coughs followed, then the sound of men running for the door. The warrior waited until he heard the door latch clicking, then raced onto the balcony. A fresh magazine was in the AR-15, and he poured half of it into the men grouped at the door.

Return fire from outside shattered windows, knocked pillows off sofas and chewed splinters from the fireplace mantel. It hit neither Bolan nor Don Salvador. The Executioner pointed back into the bedroom.

"Don Salvador, can you tie something white to what's left of the window frame? That's the signal to Angelita."

"Very well."

Don Salvador had just retreated when bullets slammed into the balcony railing. Bolan waited until he could sight on the muzzle-flashes, estimated that he faced two SMGs, then decided to use one of his grenades.

His throw was almost accurate, but "almost" didn't count in combat. The grenade struck a jutting section of window frame, bounced back into the living room and exploded there. Shrapnel ripped the bodies, but not the subgunners outside.

Without rising, Bolan dragged a bench on the balcony to the head of the stairs, then wedged it crosswise in place. The gunners outside fired several times at the noise, but only hit the bench. The warrior picked a couple of splinters out of his hand, then withdrew to the bedroom.

"I've blocked the stairs," he told Don Salvador. "If you can watch for Angelita—"

"It will be time for my insulin in the next hour," the old man said. "Do you think we'll be out of here by then?"

"If we aren't, you won't be needing insulin ever again."

"Rather what I thought," Lirio said.

In the next moment Salvador Lirio's chances of needing his next dose of insulin shrank. A large cylindrical object flew through one of the living-room windows, and Bolan had just time to smell gasoline before the room erupted in flames.

Bolan stopped worrying about covering the head of the stairs. He slammed the door and started stuffing the cracks under and around it with the handiest pieces of cloth, which happened to be Danny Lipardo's clothes.

"It seems we may have to wait outside, after all," Don Salvador observed. "In that case, may I offer you Mr. Lipardo's gun? I will need both hands for climbing, and I think you can use it more accurately, in any case."

Bolan thrust the weapon into his belt and unlatched the window sash. He looked in both directions along the rear wall of the lodge, but saw no one.

"It looks as if they're expecting the fire to drive us around to the front." He gripped Lirio's arm. "I'll lower you down first. Then—"

Bolan's tactical planning was interrupted by the sound of a helicopter approaching at low altitude—but approaching from the *front* of the lodge. The rotor noise was joined by another sound—a heavy truck, coming uphill fast.

Bolan remembered the old adage about no battle plan ever surviving contact with the enemy. Angelita had somehow managed to return at the same moment as a group of hardmen.

The Executioner scrambled out the window, up onto the dormer and from there to the peak of the roof, slamming a fresh magazine into the AR-15 while on the move.

Smoke was pouring from every window in the front of the lodge. The shingles beneath the warrior's feet were intact, but soon they'd be ablaze. But at least the flames were doing some good—the light generated by the fire enabled Bolan to see the truck growling up the hill and the landing lights of the JetRanger, which was flying just above the vehicle.

Then hardmen concealed behind the woodshed opened fire, slamming bullets into the truck's windshield and tires. Realization suddenly swept through Bolan. The truck wasn't bringing reinforcements. Fredo Guzman or the Justice Department agents had finally arrived on the scene.

They weren't going to penetrate the perimeter, and Angelita had realized that. She was flying low as a diversion, but if her diversion succeeded, she was going to be taking close-range automatic fire.

The AR-15 was bucking in Bolan's hands before he completed the thought. He shot one man who was behind the woodshed and was tracking onto several others beneath the cars when a gunner in another position opened up. He fired something heavy, on full automatic, and Bolan heard slugs smack into the helicopter. Angelita was in trouble.

He clamped down hard on any thought of the captain and turned his own weapon on the base of the line of tracer. It stopped as suddenly as it began, just as the blazing helicopter began to tilt. It went on tilting until it lost lift. Failing rotors chopped the tops of trees a hundred yards downhill, then the flames gushed up as the JetRanger crashed.

The crash was echoed as the battered truck rammed the blazing Cherokee. The smaller vehicle flew into the air, then landed squarely on top of a fleeing hardman. Another gunner ran from cover, firing from the hip, and Bolan shot him down. A third man ran toward the trees, and automatic-weapons fire from the cab and rear of the truck punched him to the ground.

Bolan slung his rifle, cupped his hands and shouted. "Guzman, up here! The rest are yours. I've got to get Salvador Lirio out."

Guzman's head jerked up at Bolan's voice, but he knew enough not to look around in a firefight. He and what looked like three or four men in hunting shirts and jeans spread out, weapons ready, to begin a thorough search of the grounds for survivors.

Bolan thought he heard at least one burst of gunfire, but he was too busy lowering Salvador Lirio out the window to pay much attention to anything else. As he climbed out himself, the bedroom door blew in, and a wave of flame and hot gas nearly hurled the warrior out the window.

The fall jammed the AR-15, so Bolan was holding the Combat Magnum as he led the old man around the end of the lodge. They had to duck falling shingles all the way, and just as they sighted Fredo Guzman, the roof of the lodge fell in.

Guzman was sitting on the bullet-punctured hood, reloading his Uzi.

"Hello, gentleman. I think we've got them all, but there's another carload of our people at the foot of the hill in case we didn't. Sorry about Angelita, though."

"What . . . ?" Lirio began.

"Angelita was trying to draw fire from the truck by flying low," Bolan said. "She succeeded, but . . . she crashed."

"In flames?" Lirio asked. His face was a blank mask.

Bolan couldn't lie. "It looked that way. But the fuel tanks were pretty low. She might have—"

"Don't hold out hope where there is none, Mr. Bruning. Let's go and find her body."

"Ah, Don Salvador . . ." Guzman began.

The pain had hit now; it showed in the old man's face and his voice as he replied. "I'm not a coward or so weak in the stomach that I can't look at Angelita's body. If I am, she will know it. Then, when we meet again, as we shall before long, she will turn away from me. I fear that judgment more than God's.''

Without waiting for anyone else, Salvador Lirio started downhill toward the crash site. Bolan took two steps after him, then stopped cold.

Now that his hearing had recovered from the firefight and he was away from the house, he could hear sounds from the forest. One of those sounds was, unmistakably, someone swearing in Spanish. A woman swearing in Spanish.

This time Salvador Lirio didn't get there first. Bolan was the first to reach the foot of the pine tree where Angelita hung. Guzman was right behind him.

''We thought you were dead!'' Guzman exclaimed.

''It was close enough,'' Angelita replied in between grunts and the sound of tearing cloth. ''I figured that the trees would break some of my fall, so I jumped just before the main tank blew. There wasn't much to blow, but I wouldn't have wanted to be any closer when it did.''

''Are you all right?''

More ripping cloth, then a rustling and a thump as the woman dropped to the ground.

''I am now. I got hung up by my harness in this damned tree.''

Angelita Lirio got to her feet, black with smoke and with the hair on the back of her head a lot shorter than it had been. In the process of getting out of the helicopter and then the tree, she'd also got lost most of her clothes.

Her grandfather approached, unbelting his dressing gown. ''Here, Angelita.''

"Grandfather, you'll freeze."

Salvador Lirio laughed and finished stripping off the dressing gown. Under it he wore blue silk pajamas. A closer look told Bolan that under the pajamas he was wearing a grey jogging suit.

"They didn't notice that I was wearing this, any more than they noticed the gun." Lirio laughed. "Fredo, if you ever take up crime, remember to search old men as thoroughly as you do young ones."

Angelita pulled on her grandfather's dressing gown. "Also, don't ever get a helicopter pilot pissed at you. They have ways of dropping in on you unexpectedly."

Then her voice broke, and she ran to her grandfather. She was several inches taller than he was, and her first hug lifted him right off his feet.

Bolan and Guzman walked off to give the Lirios privacy. For the first time since they'd been working together, Bolan noticed that the policeman looked tired.

"Did you take care of Lipardo's men in the truck?" Bolan asked.

"The Justice Department people arranged for an APB on large purchases of weapons, ammo or food. Once we got word, we looked at a map and arranged a roadblock on the way to the lodge. The truck got up past the guards at the foot of the hill, but those goons up here made us. We'd have been burned worse than Angelita if she hadn't put her tail on the line for us."

"Tell her that yourself," Bolan suggested. Guzman had left out some of the details, such as what had happened to the men in the truck, but the Executioner wasn't going to be nosy. How Guzman handled known criminals was none of his concern.

Epilogue

In the sunset light streaming through the blinds, Mack Bolan read the telegram twice, then handed it back to Angelita.

"Is your grandfather serious about making Pedro Martinez head of the Instituto de Fraternidad?"

"It won't be final until he's talked with the rest of the board. But yes, I think he's serious. That means he's going to either talk the board around or pull the plug on them and appoint Martinez on his own."

"That wouldn't be good for morale."

"No, but you have to understand my grandfather. He's decided to make a public peace with the Martinez family, and what better way than appointing old Don Luis's favorite son head of the institute?

"But my grandfather's also still a little bit of a dictator at heart. The Martinez family is going to get peace shoved down their throats and like it."

Bolan wondered if that was likely to start the old feud up again rather than heal it. Then he decided that it wasn't his problem, even if Don Salvador didn't solve it. The warrior had a feeling, though, that the old man was probably a match for the whole Martinez family put together.

Angelita put the telegram on the side table, walked over to the window, and pulled the blinds. As she walked back to the bed, she tossed her dressing gown aside, then her nightgown.

Bolan had been surprised at first to find this hunger in her. Then he realized that it was a hunger for healing as much as anything else.

For the battle against Hector Gurrola and his soldiers, Angelita had needed the Executioner. For healing the wounds of that battle, she had Sergeant Mercy.

DON PENDLETON's
MACK BOLAN®

More SuperBolan bestseller action! Longer than the monthly series, SuperBolans feature Mack in more intricate, action-packed plots— more of a good thing

Phoenix Force—bonded in secrecy to avenge the acts of terrorists everywhere

SEARCH AND DESTROY $3.95   [ ]
American "killer" mercenaries are involved in a KGB plot to
overthrow the government of a South Pacific island. The
American President, anxious to preserve his country's image and
not disturb the precarious position of the island nation's
government, sends in the experts—Phoenix Force—to prevent a
coup.

FIRE STORM $3.95   [ ]
An international peace conference turns into open warfare when
terrorists kidnap the American President and the premier of the
USSR at a summit meeting. As a last desperate measure Phoenix
Force is brought in—for if demands are not met, a plutonium
core device is set to explode.

Total Amount	$ _____
Plus 75¢ Postage	_____ .75
Payment enclosed	$ _____

Please send a check or money order payable to Gold Eagle Books.

In the U.S.	In Canada
Gold Eagle Books	Gold Eagle Books
3010 Walden Ave.	P.O. Box 609
Box 1325	Fort Erie, Ontario
Buffalo, NY 14269-1325	L2A 5X3

Please Print

Name: _____

Address: _____

City: _____

State/Prov: _____

Zip/Postal Code: _____

SPF-AR